whatever you do. don't look down!

I jerked straight up in the saddle.

"You need to stay awake," Jonathan warned. "Look to your left."

Rubbing my eye, I looked to the left . . . and froze.

We were on a cliff.

And it dropped straight down.

Hundreds, *thousands* of feet down. I couldn't even see the bottom.

Not moving a muscle in my body, I stared at the ledge we were on. Each time one of Diablo's hoofs came down, pebbles skidded over the edge and disappeared.

With my heart galloping, I inched my head to the right . . . and froze.

Another drop-off.

A really, really, *really* big drop-off.

"J-J-Jonathan?"

"Calm down, GiGi. Diablo knows what he's doing. Concentrate on not moving. Don't do anything to set him off balance."

Locking every muscle in my body, I stared hard at the black hairs of Diablo's mane. I concentrated on not moving, not breathing. I heard a short, choppy, shallow intake of air and realized it was me. Squeezing my eyes shut, I forced a swallow, trying to moisten my mouth. I'd rather see darkness than the reality of the minuscule ledge and the vast jungle around me.

I heard another choppy breath come in and out of my mouth and then a deafening roar. "What was that?"

other books you may enjoy

Alex Rider: Stormbreaker	Anthony Horowitz
Hunted: Club Dread	Walter Sorrells
Hunted: Fake I.D.	Walter Sorrells
I Was a Non-Blonde Cheerleader	Kieran Scott
S.A.S.S.: Westminster Abby	Micol Ostow
The Specialists: Model Spy	Shannon Greenland
The Specialists: Down to the Wire	Shannon Greenland
The Specialists: The Winning Element	Shannon Greenland

the specialists

native

tongue

shannon greenland

speak

An Imprint of Penguin Group (USA) Inc.

SPEAK
Published by the Penguin Group
Penguin Group (USA) Inc., 345 Hudson Street, New York, New York 10014, U.S.A.
Penguin Group (Canada), 90 Eglinton Avenue East, Suite 700,
Toronto, Ontario, Canada M4P 2Y3 (a division of Pearson Penguin Canada Inc.)
Penguin Books Ltd, 80 Strand, London WC2R 0RL, England
Penguin Ireland, 25 St Stephen's Green, Dublin 2, Ireland (a division of Penguin Books Ltd)
Penguin Group (Australia), 250 Camberwell Road, Camberwell, Victoria 3124, Australia
(a division of Pearson Australia Group Pty Ltd)
Penguin Books India Pvt Ltd, 11 Community Centre,
Panchsheel Park, New Delhi - 110 017, India
Penguin Group (NZ), 67 Apollo Drive, Rosedale, North Shore 0632, New Zealand
(a division of Pearson New Zealand Ltd)
Penguin Books (South Africa) (Pty) Ltd, 24 Sturdee Avenue,
Rosebank, Johannesburg 2196, South Africa

Registered Offices: Penguin Books Ltd, 80 Strand, London WC2R 0RL, England

Published by Speak, an imprint of Penguin Group (USA) Inc., 2008

10 9 8 7 6 5 4 3 2 1

LIBRARY OF CONGRESS CATALOGING-IN-PUBLICATION DATA
Greenland, Shannon.
The specialists : native tongue / by Shannon Greenland.
p. cm.
Summary: Computer genius GiGi is paired with Parrot, an expert linguist, on a secret mission
to South America, trying to keep a legendary piece of pottery from falling into the wrong hands.
ISBN 978-0-14-241160-5 (pbk. : alk. paper)
[1. Spies—Fiction. 2. Orphans—Fiction. 3. Genius—Fiction. 4. South America—Fiction.]
I. Title. II. Title; Native tongue.
PZ7.G8458Spn 2008   [Fic]—dc22

Speak ISBN 978-0-14-241160-5

Printed in the United States of America

dedication

A big, BIG, smooch to Tara for being, hands down, the best critique partner I could ask for. Love ya, girl!

Acknowledgments

A HUGE thanks goes to Britta, Shelly, and Tara for helping me plot this book.

A smile goes to Rob for talking vehicles with me.

And to Sara, Anita, and Jeanine for giving me Native American guidance.

the specialists

native

tongue

darren stared at the door to his grandmother's apartment. He'd been living with her for seven years, ever since his mom left, and every day it was the same thing. He'd come home from school, and she'd be sleeping on the couch.

Maybe today would be different.

Not likely.

Taking a deep breath, he turned the knob on the front door and walked in. Grandmother never locked anything. Nobody on the reservation did. That sense of trust always brought Darren peace.

As he passed through the shadowed living room toward his bedroom, he glanced at the corner where the worn-through couch sat, where his grandmother always was.

Her skinny body lay half on/half off the couch. One leg and arm dangled over the side. Her gray braid trailed across a cushion.

No matter how hard he tried, he couldn't conjure up a good memory of his grandmother. There had to be one somewhere in the recesses of his brain. Perhaps one day he'd recall it and know that she'd loved him, that she'd been happy.

Setting down his backpack, Darren crossed the living room to the couch, and stopped.

He studied her.

Breathing. She wasn't breathing.

Darren tentatively reached forward and placed his hand on her cheek.

Cold.

He slid his fingers to her chest right where her heart should beat.

Silently, he waited, holding his breath, every sense in his body tuned to his palm against her chest.

No beat.

Darren pushed away and stood over her, staring down at her lifeless form. No thoughts occupied his mind.

He waited for his body to react with tears, sickness, sadness . . .

But there was nothing. No emotion at all. Only the familiar emptiness in his heart.

Without a last glance in her direction, he gathered his things, walked from the apartment to the stables down the road, jumped onto his horse—his only friend in the world—and rode bareback across the Arizona desert toward the sun.

⸭ ⸭ ⸭

"*Vuv,*" Talon commanded two days later. Sit.

Darren sat on a low wooden stool across from his tribal chief.

Between them a fire flickered in a shallow, stone pit. The smoke trailed upward out of a special opening in the roof.

Darren had never understood Talon's penchant for heat. It could be one hundred degrees outside and he'd still have a fire burning. Although Talon lived in an ordinary one-story home, he spent all his time in this added-on room built to seem like something from a century ago. Animal skulls hung on the walls, and skins covered the floor. A few pieces of roughly made wood furniture sat scattered about.

Talon puffed his pipe and then extended it, keeping his black, heartless eyes level on Darren.

Sharing a smoke with an elder was a great privilege, one any teenage male would jump at. Darren had tried it a few times and ended up coughing for days afterward. So now he preferred not to do it at all.

Talon knew this, yet repeatedly offered Darren the pipe. It was one of the many reasons he had no respect for the tribal chief.

With a grunt, Talon indicated the hand-carved pipe.

Darren shook his head.

Talon's lips sneered, as if he got some twisted amusement from the pipe game.

Darren hated coming to this room. The whole place had a wicked aura. *Talon* had a wicked aura.

Straightening his back, the tribal chief placed his palms on his knees. Barefoot and without a shirt, he wore only a pair of dark jeans.

"Yjoto jixo aae doop?" Where have you been? Talon asked.

"Vjo enuhhu." The cliffs. Darren would still be there if not for his grandmother's funeral ceremony tomorrow.

Someone knocked softly on the door and then quietly opened it, sending in cooler air from the main house. Talon's oldest daughter entered, head bowed, and shuffled across the floor to where Talon and Darren sat.

Darren had never heard any of Talon's daughters speak, or Talon's wife for that matter. They all looked the same, with long skirts, blouses, and braided hair. And they always shuffled around with their heads bowed.

The daughter knelt beside Talon and picked up a tray with the remains of his dinner. As she stood, he grabbed her arm and yanked her to him. The tray thudded to the floor.

"Nov jot ia!" Let her go!

Both Talon and his daughter snapped surprised eyes toward Darren, as if neither could believe someone actually had the nerve to speak up against Talon, to defend a female.

He'd witnessed Talon treat other women harshly, too. And the women never fought back. In one way the subservience annoyed Darren. Why did the women allow themselves to be treated like that? Why wouldn't they just leave? The reservation had no iron gates, anybody could walk off at any time.

Darren's mother had.

In another way the situation irritated him. Actually, it ticked him off. What gave Talon or any man the right to treat women like that? Did it boost his ego? It didn't do that for Darren. It made him physically ill.

With a sardonic chuckle, the chief shoved his daughter away. She quickly picked up the tray and scurried out of the room.

Talon placed a small log on the fire, making the flames grow. Shadows flickered off his Mohawk and his chest.

Evil and *dark*, two words Darren had always associated with the chief.

Talon rubbed his fingers over the thick, black stripes tattooed down his chin. "*Auet itipfoavjot uu foif.*" Your grandmother is dead.

"*U mpay.*" I know.

"*Jot eotooapa uu vaoattay.*" Her ceremony is tomorrow.

Darren wiped a trail of sweat from his cheek. "*Unn do vjoto.*" I'll be there.

Silence fell between them as they stared at each other in the dim light.

All he wanted to do was get on his horse and ride, fast and hard. Anywhere. Everywhere. His horse had been and would always be his refuge. But out of respect for his mother, he would attend the ceremony.

Talon cleared his throat and spit into the fire. "You will stay here," he said, switching to English, "in your grandmother's apartment."

No way. Darren had already thought about it. He was leaving as soon as Grandmother's ceremony ended. "I've made other plans."

The chief chuckled low and humorlessly. "What plans? You are seventeen. You have no money."

It didn't matter. Darren would live in the cliffs, the mountains, the woods, any place but here. "I've made other plans."

Talon ran his tongue across his teeth. "You have a unique gift. The gods chose you. You must repay the gods by honoring your blood."

Even in the overheated room, Darren's body chilled. "What do you mean?"

"Your tongue is magic."

Darren had never told anyone about his special ability. His grandmother must have opened her mouth. But not even *she* knew the extent of his gift.

No one did.

You keep this a secret, Darren's mother had made him promise. *Not until you're grown and gone, old enough to have wisdom, do you tell anybody of your talent. People will expoit it if they have the chance.*

He remembered how she'd play a tape in another language, and he'd mimic the speech. They'd laugh. It was a childhood game. One he often thought of fondly.

"My tongue is like anyone else's," Darren lied.

"I have a job for you. It pays well."

"Not interested."

The chief grunted. "You will be."

Not likely.

"The Uopoei Nation does great business. International. Thirty-one countries now. You will translate transactions. Interpret the meetings."

"No thanks."

"It's important business. There's a lot of honor that goes with being involved."

Illegal, I'm sure. "I said no."

Talon smirked as he took a small poker from the fire and touched it to his pipe. "I know where your mother is."

Hope surged through Darren. Talon knew Darren would do anything for that information. "Where?"

The chief puffed his pipe three times. "*Aae fu lad. U vonn aae xjoto aaet oavjot uu.*" You work for me, and I'll tell you where your mother is.

▥ ▥ ▥

SQUINTING AGAINST THE VENEZUELAN SUN. Darren watched a plane touch down on the deserted runway.

Why did these business transactions always take place in the middle of nowhere?

Two weeks ago he'd been in a Russian forest.

Three weeks ago it'd been the Swedish mountains.

Last week it was a boat in China.

Never once had Darren seen "the cargo." Nor had anybody called it anything other than "the cargo." And Talon never came with Darren on these trips.

Something illegal was definitely going on.

Darren cared, sure he cared.

But he cared more about finding his mother.

Six months, Darren reminded himself. That was what he and Talon had agreed upon. Six months and he'd know where his mother was.

The big guy beside Darren adjusted his dark sunglasses. *"Esta supuesto ser el mejor cargamento."* Supposed to be the best cargo yet.

Darren didn't know the guy's name. Nobody knew anyone else's name. All Darren knew was what languages to speak. Today it'd be Spanish and German.

The plane pulled past them, pushing a warm, fuel-scented gust of wind across the runway. Holding on to his cowboy hat, the South American guy led the way over the packed dirt to where the plane stopped.

The back of it slowly lowered, and a man and a woman walked out, both blond and dressed in white business suits. Behind them in the plane's belly sat a huge silver crate, big enough to hold livestock.

The cargo.

Cowboy-Hat Guy nodded to the man and the woman. *"Bienvenidos."* Welcome. *"¿Todo está listo?"* Is everything ready?

"Wilkommen. Ist alles fertig?" Darren translated to the German couple.

The woman glanced beyond him to the semitruck that Cowboy-Hat Guy had driven and the motorcycle Darren rode. *"Haben Sie unser Geld?"* Do you have our money?

As soon as the money and the cargo exchanged hands, everyone would go their separate ways. Darren never knew where "the cargo" ended up.

"*¿Tienes nuestro dinero?*" He interpreted for Cowboy-Hat Guy.

Cowboy lifted the brown leather duffel bag he held in his left hand.

The woman descended the metal ramp leading from the plane and took the duffel bag.

And then everything happened in a blur.

Cowboy threw the woman to the ground and drew a gun on the blond man. "*¡Policía! No se muevan.*" Police! Don't move.

The doors to the semi banged open. Out jumped a squad of guys with machine guns. They raced across the tarmac and up the ramp into the plane.

A squad guy handcuffed the blond man.

Cowboy handcuffed the woman.

Before Darren had time to think, move, or breathe, he was thrown to the ground and handcuffed, too.

Two guys smashed the padlocks on the silver crate, opened the doors, and stepped back.

Nobody said a word.

Darren kept his gaze glued to the crate. From the shadows stumbled a young girl, maybe twelve, dressed in ragged clothes. Then another came out, even younger, dressed the same. And then another.

The cargo.

Darren's stomach rolled on a wave of nausea as girl after girl stepped from the crate. Some crying, others wide-eyed with fear. Some clung to one another while others used their hands and arms to shield the bright sun. There were about thirty in all.

A squad guy ran up the ramp carrying blankets. The girls cowered. *"Dígales que está bien. Somos la policía. Van a regresar a sus padres."* Tell them it's okay. We're the police. They're going home to their parents.

"Es ist O.K.," Darren translated to German. *"Das ist die Polizei. Sie gehen nach Hause zu ihren Eltern."*

The girls began sobbing as the police wrapped blankets around their tiny bodies. Darren swallowed as he watched the guys escort the scared girls down the ramp.

Even though he suspected the answer, Darren asked anyway, *"¿Quiénes son?"* Who are they?

"Ahora son niñas inocentes, pero esta noche habrían sido vendidas a la esclavitud." Right now they're innocent little girls, but tonight they'd have been sold into slavery.

Darren's lunch shot a burning path from his stomach. He turned and threw up.

░ ░ ░

THE COP UNLOCKED THE CELL and shoved Darren inside. He'd never been in jail before, never even seen the inside of a police station. For that matter, he'd never been in a squad car before.

Without looking around, he sat on a wooden bench to the

left. As long as he kept to himself and didn't seem scared, everyone should leave him alone.

That's what he'd told himself a hundred times since being handcuffed forty-five minutes ago.

"*¡ESTÁN AQUÍ!*" THEY'RE HERE!

Darren jumped.

A skinny man dressed in red long johns rolled out from under a bench on the other side of the cell. His wispy black hair stuck out in a million directions.

He trotted around the place, waving his arms. "*Estánaquíestánaquíestánaquíestánaquí.*"

Another cell occupant shoved the skinny man, and he stumbled across the cement straight into Darren.

His heart slammed his ribs. "Get away from me," Darren ordered in Spanish.

With blurry eyes, the skinny man grinned. "Hee-hee-hee." A rotten stench seeped from the man's mouth.

Darren held his breath.

"Hee-hee-hee." The skinny man slid past, crawled back under his bench, and curled into a tight ball.

Quietly, Darren released his breath.

The guy to his right stood up. Darren chanced a quick look. Over six feet tall, the guy had to weigh more than three hundred pounds. It was amazing the rickety bench had held his weight.

Tattoos covered every spot of his bare upper body and bald head. His black beard hung to the middle of his chest.

Definitely someone Darren did not want messing with him.

The enormous guy lumbered over to the bars. "You looking at me?" he threatened the cop sitting outside the cell.

The cop looked on, bored.

The enormous guy grabbed the bars, gave them a hard rattle, and screamed, "YOU LOOKING AT ME?"

The cop lit a cigarette and checked his watch.

He must see this crazy stuff all the time.

The enormous guy stomped back over to the bench and plopped down. Darren held on so he wouldn't fall off.

Down the hall a door unlocked, probably another crazy on the way. Darren listened intently, but heard nothing.

A few seconds later, a man dressed in a suit stepped into view. He turned and looked straight at Darren through the spookiest light green eyes he had ever seen.

Swallowing, he stared back at the man. What was going on?

The man handed the cop a letter, and the cop slowly perused it. Then he unclipped his keys from his belt and unlocked the cell. *"Vamos."* Let's go. He pointed to Darren.

Darren slowly got up, crossed the floor, and exited the cell.

The man extended his hand. "Thomas Liba. You may call me TL. Follow me, please."

Darren walked beside him down the corridor. *Thomas Liba.* Darren rolled the name around in his brain. Definitely not a Venezuelan. So who was this man? Police? A lawyer? Someone from the U.S. embassy? Whoever he was, Darren vowed to keep his mouth shut. He was only the translator, after all. He definitely wasn't going to tell TL a thing. Not with the where-abouts of his mother at stake.

The man led Darren through a small waiting room and then into a private office. Indicating two black metal chairs, TL took one and Darren sat in the other.

TL leaned down and took a file from beneath his chair. He opened it and sifted through. "Darren Yote. Seventeen years old. Six feet tall. One hundred sixty-five pounds. Black hair, black eyes. Mother's one hundred percent Native American. Father was a mixture of everything. Father died in a car accident before you were born. Mother disappeared when you were seven. Your mater-nal grandmother was your legal guardian for the past ten years."

Man, this guy knows everything about me.

"You make good grades, but never take a book home from school. The only D you ever got was in Spanish." TL glanced up at Darren. "Interesting."

Darren guiltily swallowed. He'd purposefully made that D so no one would know how good he was.

TL closed the file. "I work for the IPNC. Information Protection National Concern. I head up the Specialists, a group of brilliant, talented young men and women."

What did this man want with him?

"For the past ten years, the IPNC has been following this slave ring. We've made a lot of busts, returned numerous boys and girls back to their homes, but we can't seem to flush out the head of the operation." TL undid a button on his suit jacket and shifted in his chair. "We were all a little surprised when you popped up on the scene. Russia, China, Venezuela, Sweden. You seem to know how to speak pretty much every language."

Darren cleared his throat, but continued to remain silent. This was exactly what his mother had warned him about. All people wanted to do was take advantage of his ability. Talon had.

Quietly, TL studied Darren's face. "Do you know who's in charge of this slave ring?"

"No," Darren lied.

"I think you do. Will you tell me, please?"

"I just told you, I don't know." Darren kept his gaze steady with TL, trying not to show any emotion.

"Perhaps *you're* in charge." TL raised his brows. "Hm?"

This man knew Darren wasn't in charge, so he didn't even bother answering such an outlandish accusation.

Again, TL quietly studied him. Long minutes went by, and Darren kept returning the stare. But . . . this man, TL, wouldn't blink, wouldn't swallow, wouldn't do anything. It was the stillest Darren had ever seen someone be. And it only made him more aware of his own need to blink, to swallow.

More time passed, and with each second, Darren felt, oddly enough, as if he was being pulled into TL's mind. That TL could read Darren's own thoughts.

Swallowing, Darren glanced down at his lap, his heart racing with the uncomfortable yet somehow serene air between them.

"Does this person have something over you?" TL quietly asked.

Thoughts of Darren's mother flooded his memories, and he

felt tears press against his eyes. Clenching his jaw, he kept staring at his lap, willing away his urge to cry.

TL reached across and grabbed his shoulder. "Son, I want you to know you can trust me. I'm the good guy."

No one had ever called Darren "son" before. He lifted his gaze and stared into TL's intense eyes and knew, without a doubt, that he could trust this man. "His name's Talon, and he told me if I'd do this for him he'd reunite me with my mother."

TL nodded, taking it in. "Talon's an evil man. And evil people don't keep their word. The reality is that he never intended to reunite you with your mother."

Somewhere in the back of his mind, Darren had known that all along. But holding on to a thread of hope had kept him going, kept him doing what Talon wanted.

"And the truth is," TL continued, "*I* have the power to find your mother."

Hope surged through Darren at those words. Did this man really have the power to find his mother? He probably did if he worked for the government. They had access to all kinds of things Darren never would. But, what did TL want in return?

"In return for her whereabouts, I want you to testify against Talon," TL said, answering Darren's unspoken question.

Immediately, Darren shook his head. "No. Not until my mother is safe."

With a thoughtful sigh, TL propped his elbows on the chair's armrest. He tapped his fingers together, thinking. "Okay."

"Okay? You'll find my mother?" he asked in disbelief.

TL nodded. "Yes, but on one condition."

"What condition?" Darren asked, his hope slowly slipping away.

"I want you to come work for me."

Darren paused for a split second and then nodded. "Okay, but I have a condition of my own."

"Go ahead."

"I want to bring my horse with me."

1

"GIGI," Bruiser yelled. "Get your butt out here. We're dying to see you!"

Ignoring my lovable pest of a friend, I slipped a tiny silver hoop through my left earlobe and took a step back. I scrutinized my appearance in the oversize mirror mounted above the sinks.

I went down the list that Cat had taped to the corner of the mirror.

Blond hair, loose. Check.

Clear lip gloss. Check.

Shine-proof powder. Check.

Black eyeliner on the bottom lid. Check.

Low-rise dark-wash jeans. Check.

Black ballet flats. Check.

Black leather belt. Check.

Light blue, snug, sleeveless sweater, not tucked. Check.

Matching bra and thong, the tan set. Check.

Cat and I had argued about the last item. What did it matter what color underwear I wore? I didn't intend on David seeing it. But Cat insisted it was more of a confidence booster.

Loosening my belt a hole, I took a deep breath. David and I were about to go on our first "official" date. My first date ever.

Was that sad?

Although David did take me to the fair for my sixteenth birthday last year, the night before I got busted by the IPNC. But the fair thing hadn't been a date. I didn't even know he liked me back then. His taking me to the fair had all been a setup leading to my arrest. It truly was hard to believe it had all happened nearly a year ago.

It seemed as if we'd been trying to get to this dating point forever. With school, the Specialists missions, bad guys, training, and any number of other things, David and I barely had time to say hello to each other.

I'm exaggerating, of course, but it sure felt like it sometimes.

Wait a minute. Back up. Lip gloss? I ran my finger over my bottom lip. This stuff would totally come off when we kissed. It'd get all over David. He didn't want slimy lips. No one wanted slimy lips.

I rushed across the tile and wrenched open the door. "Cat, my lip glo—" My kissing issue trailed away as I took in the crowd in our bedroom.

Bruiser rolled off her bed. "It's about time. I was going gray waiting on you." She whistled. "Yowza, babe."

Smiling, I stepped into the room.

Mystic sat on his favorite spot of carpet at the foot of Bruiser's bed. He always sat there when he hung out in the girls' room.

He gave me a quick once-over. "I do believe the moon is in the second house and Jupiter's aligned with Mars."

Huh?

"Don't listen to Psychic Guy. That's from a song. He's being a goof. You're hot." Bruiser bopped Mystic in the back of the head. "Tell her she's hot."

Mystic rubbed his head. "All right, all right. You're hot."

I laughed.

Stretched out across her bed, Beaker brought her nose out from her chemistry book. She stopped chomping her gum and playfully smirked her black lipstick—covered lips. "Yeah, you'll do."

After all the rockiness between Beaker and me, we'd gained an appreciation of each other. Our mission a month ago to Barracuda Key, Florida, had shown me a side of her I never would have guessed existed. Plus, I'd learned to dig her ever-changing hair. Orange was this week's color. It matched the gem in her nose and the ones in her dog collar.

And I still found it amazing that she and David were half brother and sister. Which meant if David and I ever got married, Beaker and I would be . . . sisters?

A month ago I would've gagged at the thought. But now it merely hit me as interesting. Beaker and me sisters. Hmmm. Not that David and I were getting married or anything. I'm jumping ahead. *Way* ahead. We needed to get through our first date.

Parrot reclined on my bed propped up with my pillows. "You look beautiful, GiGi."

My nervous jitters relaxed with his heartfelt compliment. "Thanks, Parrot."

Parrot always said the sweetest, most meaningful things. Whatever girl snagged him would be very, very lucky.

Wirenut winked as he popped a potato chip in his mouth. "Whadaya say you ditch David? You and I'll hit the town. I'll show you how to hot-wire a car."

Lying beside him, Cat elbowed Wirenut in the ribs. "You better be glad I love you. Besides, you know I can hot-wire better than you."

He grinned and planted a hard kiss on her lips. With their olive skin and black hair, they looked like those couples who always dressed alike. They totally belonged together.

She climbed over him and crossed the carpet to me. "Looks like you followed the list. Now what were you going to ask me about lip gloss?"

I glanced over her shoulder to our packed bedroom. Everyone's eyes were silently glued to me. I leaned in and whispered, "Won't the gloss gross David out when we kiss?"

I felt silly asking Cat the question, but it wasn't like I'd kissed a whole heck of a lot of guys. I didn't have any experience to draw on. Every other time David and I had kissed I hadn't been wearing anything on my lips.

Her amber eyes twinkled, and she smiled. "David's really not going to care."

Bruiser loudly cleared her throat. "It's rude to whisper."

Cat squeezed my arm. "Relax. Have fun. And by all means do *not* think about anything back here at the ranch."

"Thanks for all your help getting ready." I hugged her. "There's no telling what I'd look like right now without your list."

It reminded me of my first mission. The modeling instructor had written me list after list so I'd know what to wear every day. So I'd know what made a good outfit. Pathetic, but completely true. I had no sense of style.

Someone knocked on the bedroom door. *David.* My stomach dippity-dipped.

Bruiser boinged onto her bed and flipped off the other side. "Why, whoever could that be?" She swung the door open and checked her watch. "You're one minute late."

David laughed, playfully pushed her out of the way, and came the rest of the way in. He stopped suddenly, his eyes touching each person in the room. "Didn't realize this was a family affair."

"Yep, family affair." Wirenut swung his legs over the bed and got up. "If GiGi had parents, they'd be here to greet you and give you the third degree."

Bruiser went to stand beside Wirenut and put her hands on her hips. "Tonight we're your third degree."

David looked across the room at me. I shrugged. I mean really, what was I supposed to do? Shove past them? Plus, it gave me a moment to slurp up his yumminess.

Disheveled dark hair. Stubble on his face. Perfect, not-too-tight, not-too-loose jeans. Black shoes. Black shirt. I *loved* when he wore black.

Other than our shirts, we matched perfectly.

Wirenut ran his fingers down his trim goatee. "What are your plans for this evening, young man?"

David held a smile back. "Food and the Boardwalk."

Bruiser flipped a red braid over her shoulder. "We don't approve of underage drinking."

"Yes, ma'am."

Wirenut took a chip from his bag and ate it. "Do you smoke?"

"No, sir."

"Her curfew is midnight. One minute past and . . ." Bruiser held her T-shirt out. It read YOU MESS WITH MY FAMILY AND YOU MESS WITH ME.

Bruiser and her silly shirts. And the fact that Bruiser was acting the role of my mother was hilarious—especially since she was the youngest one of us all.

David nodded. "Oh, yes ma'am."

Wirenut tossed yet another chip in his mouth. "What kind of vehicle do you drive?"

"I've got a truck tonight."

"A truck?" Bruiser wagged her finger. "I don't want any of that business of her sitting in the middle getting cozy with you."

Bruiser!

She wagged her finger again. "I want both of you in a seat belt."

"Yes, ma'am."

Another chip for Wirenut. "What about your future, son? You going to be able to support our little girl someday?"

Wirenut! Sheesh.

Bruiser patted Wirenut's shoulder. "Now, honey, it's their first date. Let's see where things go."

"Yes, yes, quite right." Wirenut glanced down at Bruiser. "Anything else, Momma?"

Bruiser shook her head. "I believe that's it, Daddy."

My "father" motioned me on. "All right, this young man seems suitable."

"Oh, thank God. No telling what you would've said next," I said, laughing.

I snatched my purse from my dresser and strode across the girls' room to where David stood. His cologne moseyed through my senses. *Gggrrr.*

"Oh, and one last thing," Bruiser called out. "Don't forget our mother/daughter discussion on birth control. We don't want any more little geniuses running around."

My face caught on fire. Everyone in the room busted out laughing, like they'd all been waiting for that last comment.

The twerps.

David grabbed my hand and tugged me out the door. "Ignore them."

"I can't *believe* she said that." No, actually, I could. Bruiser was ornery that way.

"They wouldn't pick on you if they didn't love you."

True. And I loved them, too.

David led me down the hall past the other bedrooms, TL's office, and the hidden elevator that led to the underground rooms.

My embarrassment faded as I tuned in to the guy beside me. I was going on my first date. And not with some loser either. I had a really hot, funny, sweet, awesome guy.

We passed the cafeteria and stopped in the archway to the common area. TL reclined in an oversize comfy chair, reading the paper.

David knocked on the wall. "Wanted to let you know we're out of here."

TL glanced up. "Be back by midnight."

David and I nodded.

"You two look good." TL went back to his paper. "Be safe."

David opened the front door, letting in the slightly muggy night. "I should have told you that first."

"What?" I slid my purse up my shoulder.

"You look good." David's eyes slowly roamed down my body and back up. "*Real* nice."

I *loved* when he did that eye-roaming thing. It totally turned me on and made me feel sexy.

"Too good you look." I shook my head. "I mean, you look good, too."

Sigh. Not so sexy after all.

He laughed and gave me a swift kiss. "You're adorable."

"I'm glad someone thinks so." *You're dorky is more like it.*

TL's full-size truck sat parked in the circular driveway. David opened the door for me and then went around to the driver's side.

He climbed in and stretched his arm along the seat back. "Come 'ere."

I unbuckled my seat belt and slid across, more than happy to oblige him. "Bruiser said not to do this."

David smiled. "I'll never tell." He looked at my lips. "I figured we'd better toast."

"Toast?"

"Here's to us not getting a call from TL."

"I'll *definitely* toast to that." My cell had been *way* too active lately.

David leaned in and kissed me. Long and dreamy. Slow. Taking all the time in the world. He tasted minty. Every time we kissed I swore it was the best one yet. But this one topped the rest.

He pulled back. "We could sit here the whole night and keep making out."

Laughing, I glanced at his shiny mouth, and my amusement died. It looked like he'd been eating greasy fried chicken.

"My lip gloss," I realized aloud. Oh no.

"What?" David wiped his hand over his mouth and then checked out his fingers.

I grabbed his slimy hand and rubbed it on my jeans. "I'm so sorry." *I'm an idiot.*

"GiGi," he chuckled, stilling my hand.

Wait. If he looked that greasy I had to look the same or worse. I yanked the rearview mirror over and checked out my face. "I'm sorry." I fumbled with the glove compartment, found a napkin, and scrubbed away the mess. "I *knew* this lip gloss thing was not a good idea," I mumbled.

Cramming the napkin in my jacket pocket, I turned to him.

His eyes crinkled. "You done freaking out?"

"Did that gross you out?"

David softly rubbed my earlobe between his thumb and finger. "Nothing about you grosses me out."

I leaned into his hand. "Thanks."

With another quick kiss, he started the engine. "Seat belt."

"Oh." I scooted to my side and strapped in.

David pulled away from the ranch house, and I reached inside my purse for the lip gloss. Maybe I should have him turn around so I could run back in and borrow Cat's stay-on stuff. It certainly made more sense—if you're going to be kissing a guy, you needed stay-on stuff. Not glossy, glistening stuff.

Surely other girls didn't obsess over whether to reapply or not. I glanced down at the tube, and the spiral swirl of the gloss made me think of the eteus code I'd been working on earlier today. It had the same pattern.

Now if I squared the last number, then multiplied by the root of the one hundred and eighth term, I could quadruple . . . no, that would be countably infini—

"What are you thinking about?" David drove through the

[26]

ranch's gates. On the visor's remote he typed in his personal code, and the gates closed.

But if I stacked the numerical order and isolated the j—

"GiGi?"

"Huh?"

David turned onto the highway. "You're on a date, remember? At least pretend you're having fun."

"I'm sorry. I am having fun." I was on a date with the greatest guy in the world, and he didn't think I was having fun. I sucked at this.

He reached across the cab and took my hand. "Tell me what's bothering you so we can fix it and have a good time tonight."

"Who says something's bothering me?"

David squeezed my fingers. "I'm waiting."

"You know me too well," I grumbled. "Lip gloss or eteus code. Take your pick."

"Let's go for lip gloss."

I held up the tube. "Do you want me to put more on or leave it off?"

"The lip gloss is pretty if you're not going to be kissing someone. But I intend to kiss you at least a billion times tonight. My vote is that you leave it off."

"A billion?"

He caressed his thumb along my hand and smiled. "Possibly a trillion. Good thing you're a genius. Not many girls can count to a trillion."

We both laughed, and the eteus code and lip gloss issues effectively faded away. That was one thing I liked about David. He knew the perfect things to say to lighten a moment.

Twenty fantastic, conversational minutes later, we pulled into the Boardwalk's packed parking lot. The Boardwalk stretched three miles along San Belden, California's coast. Amusement rides, food, dancing, Roller-Blading—you name it, the place had it. It never closed down.

David cut the lights and engine. "Don't you dare open that door."

I held my hands up.

He came around and opened it—very gentleman-like—and I climbed out. Closing the door, he pinned me against the truck and rained kisses over my forehead, my eyes, cheeks, lips, chin, and ears. He moved to my neck and nibbled a path down one side and up the other.

Pressing a kiss to my nose, he stepped back. "I hope you were counting because that covered a big chunk of the trillion."

"Thirty-six," I breathed.

He looked at me. "You *did* count?"

"Yes. Wasn't I supposed to?"

David laughed and took my hand. "Come on."

We wound our way through the sea of vehicles until we stood on the Boardwalk's edge. My stomach grumbled at the smell of fried food.

He gazed right and then left. "Where do you want to start?"

"Food." I hadn't eaten since this morning. "Can we get a hot dog?" Something about the carnival atmosphere made me want one.

"You can have anything you want."

We joined the crowd moving up and down the Boardwalk. Men, women, couples, families, and others our age. Black, white, Hispanic, Asian. Fat, skinny, short, tall. Pierced, tattooed, or plain.

Unique people packed the place. I'd never seen anything like it.

Latin music poured from a flashing nightclub. I glanced in the open doors as we passed. Bodies gyrated to the pulsing sound.

David led me through the crowd over to a hot-dog stand. "How do you want yours?"

"Relish." I normally ordered onions, too. But with the trillion kisses . . .

We took our hot dogs to a vacant bench. With the beach and ocean at our backs, we ate, watching the crowd shuffle by.

There was something meditative about people-watching. Hearing them talk, seeing them laugh, observing their body language. TL taught a whole class on it back at the ranch. It was easy to see who felt happy, who was sad, who had hidden secrets.

"Hiii, Daaavid," two girls flirted, coming toward us.

I recognized them from the university. Their perfection reminded me of all those girls who used to make fun of me back in Iowa, before I joined the Specialists.

They gave me a polite, fake smile. I shoved the last bite of hot dog in my mouth, and relish dripped onto my blue sweater.

I stared at the green clump and oddly enough didn't feel embarrassed. I felt relieved, glad to get it over with. I knew my klutziness would come out at some point.

One of them giggled. That would've intimidated me at one time, made me feel even more awkward. Now it only fueled my self-worth. I mean, really, who cared if I dropped relish? No one was perfect.

Using my napkin, I wiped up the green clump.

"All done?" David asked.

I nodded.

Picking up my garbage, he threw our trash in the can beside the bench. "You ladies have fun tonight." He took my hand. "Let's go."

As we walked through the crowd, I glanced over my shoulder back at the two perfect girls. With matching haughtiness, they stared at our backs.

I smiled, kinda slow and la-dee-da like. *He's my date and not yours.* Rotten of me, but I'd never done that before.

Glancing over to the Ferris wheel, I skidded to a stop as Chapling and the code we'd been tinkering with popped into my brain. "Wait, I have to write this down."

"What is it?" David asked with a grin.

I ripped the notepad and pencil from my back pocket, flipped through pages and pages of code until I found my spot, and began scribbling.

"And that'll circle back around to . . ." I mumbled and continued jotting. "But then if I go this route . . ." Feverishly, I wrote code before I lost any of it. "And then Chapling won't agree so I'll have to do this. . . ." On and on I scripted until I proved every single block.

There. Holding the pad away, I studied what I'd done. Chapling was going to love this.

I jerked my eyes up. David had moved us off the Boardwalk over to the beach. I hadn't even realized we'd moved. "How long have I—"

"Ten minutes."

"Ten minutes? I'm so sorry. I saw the Ferris wheel, and it reminded me . . ." I closed my eyes and groaned. I was *such* a geek.

David tapped my forehead. "I think smart chicks are cool."

He'd said the same thing to me twice before. I opened my eyes. Behind him the Ferris wheel slowly rotated, illuminating the night sky.

A moist breeze blew in from the ocean, and I shivered.

"You're adorable." Wrapping his arms around me, he gave me a tender kiss. "That's thirty-seven."

I smiled. "Wanna ride the Ferris wheel?"

"Definitely."

And we did. We spent hours weaving our way up and down the Boardwalk. We rode rides, played games, ate cotton candy. David won me a tiny stuffed giraffe at a coin toss, and we had our picture taken in a photo booth. It was the best night of my life.

He linked fingers with me as he led me from the Boardwalk through the parking lot back to the truck. In thirty minutes it would be midnight.

"Yo, David," a group of guys called.

He waved. I recognized them from the university.

"A couple of those guys are in my physics study group." David brought our hands to his mouth and kissed the back of mine. "They're so jealous right now."

"Jealous?"

"Because I'm with the tall, hot, smart chick from the ranch."

"Tall, hot, smart chick?"

"That's what they call you."

Nobody had ever called me a tall, hot, smart chick. "What do *you* call me?"

We reached the truck. David leaned back against it and pulled me into his arms. "My girlfriend."

My heart pitter-pattered. He'd never actually called me that before. "Girlfriend?"

He squeezed me. "You don't mind do you?"

I looked into his eyes and smiled. "Umm—"

Bzzzzbzzzzbzzzz.

bzzzbzzzbzzz.

David and I pulled apart. We both glanced down at our cell phones clipped to our jeans.

* * *. TL's code to return to home base. ASAP.

David texted TL that we'd be there as quickly as possible.

I smiled a little to hide my disappointment. Sure our date was almost over, but TL's text had cut it a little short. I'd actually been enjoying myself tonight and had almost forgotten my other world. Not that I didn't like working for the Specialists, but I never really got a taste of what it was like to be a normal teenager. I felt like my life was always in mission mode.

David took my hand, obviously picking up on my bummed-out mood. "At least we just about made it through the whole date."

I nodded.

David opened the passenger door. "This is our life, GiGi. I don't know what else to say."

"I know." I climbed inside the truck. There wasn't anything else *to* say. This *was* our life.

Closing my door, David circled around to his side and hopped in. "As much as it sometimes annoys me, I wouldn't swap it for anything in the world. It's a privilege to work for the Specialists. And I'm glad I can share it with you."

I nodded, softening a little at his last statement. David always came across level-headed about this secret life we lived. I didn't know how he did it. He willingly accepted whatever happened. Never once had I seen him not be positive, not be the voice of reason. Never once had I heard him say a negative thing or express discontent.

But then he'd lived on the ranch his whole life. He didn't know anything other than this private world.

He leaned over and kissed me, caressing the back of his fingers down my cheek. "I want you to answer my question before we leave."

"What question?"

His eyes did that sexy crinkle thing. "You don't mind if I call you my girlfriend, do you?"

I didn't even try to hide the huge grin that crept onto my cheeks. "I don't mind at all."

David laughed and started the truck's engine. Any lingering melancholy drifted away as we pulled away from the Boardwalk.

▦ ▦ ▦

THIRTY MINUTES LATER, WE ENTERED the underground conference room and closed the door behind us. I wondered if TL held meetings at such weird hours as part of our training. I'd been to unexpected meetings at five in the morning, three in the afternoon, and midnight.

TL sat at the head of the long metal table with Parrot to his left. Jonathan, our physical-training instructor, sat at the other end. David rolled a leather chair out in his usual spot to the right of TL, and I made myself comfortable beside Parrot.

If history repeated itself, TL was about to take Parrot's monitoring patch. At least that was what happened with me, Wirenut, and Beaker the first time we met TL down here away from the others.

When we first got recruited by the Specialists, TL had required each of us to wear the flesh-toned tracking device. He kept tabs on us everywhere we went. Even the bathroom. I still cringed at that thought.

To my knowledge only Parrot, Mystic, and Bruiser still wore theirs. He'd taken mine, Wirenut's, and Beaker's right before sending us on our first missions.

And since I was in here with Parrot, that meant I was probably going with him.

Inwardly, I sighed, although at this point it really didn't surprise me. So much for working from home base, as TL had originally promised me.

TL closed the folder in front of him and looked up. "What can any of you tell me about the Junoesque Jungle?"

Suddenly my mind zinged back to when I was nine years old, the year I tested out of eighth grade. "We had completed a whole unit on the Junoesque Jungle in my science class," I replied. "There are three hundred species per every two acres, more than any other area in the world. Five species of plants that exist there are bougainvillea, curare, coconut tree, kapok tree, and strangler fig. Some of the animals that live there include chimpanzee, tamarin, harpy eagle, kinkajou, silvery gibbon, and toco toucan. Of course I wouldn't know a kinkajou from a gibbon if one walked right up to me and slapped me in the face."

I swept a proud smile over everyone in the conference room, then slowly realized from their perplexed looks that, once again, I'd made a complete nerd of myself.

TL's lips twitched. "Your science teacher would be proud."

Everyone chuckled, and I joined in. Joke's on me. I mean, really, what was the point of getting embarrassed? They expected this stuff from me.

"Yesterday afternoon," TL began, getting everyone back on track, "in Rutina, South America, a sixteen-year-old girl walked out from the Junoesque Jungle and onto an excavation site. She was carrying only one thing."

He pointed a remote to the wall-mounted screen behind Jonathan, and he scooted out of the way. A picture of an old vase flashed into view. "Parrot, do you know what this is?"

Parrot didn't answer at first as he studied the screen. "That can't be the Mother Nature vase." He looked at TL. "I thought that was a Native American myth."

TL nodded. "Not anymore. What do you know about it?"

"I know that it's a centuries-old artifact believed by many native tribes to control Mother Nature."

TL zoomed in on the brown, weathered pottery. "Exactly. This vase is believed to control the elements. It gives the one who holds the vase the power over nature. It is coveted by various Indian tribes." The vase rotated slowly on the screen. Cracked, and missing chunks, the vase was divided into four sections, each engraved with symbols and pictures.

TL froze the screen on one of those sections. "Notice this is a rough depiction of rain. The symbols above and below the rain are a prayer. Whatever it is a tribe needs, they say the prayer corresponding to the picture."

The vase rotated again, showing us the other roughly chiseled pictures of nature: the sun, a gust of wind, snowflakes, and again the rain.

"How big is it?" David asked.

TL referenced his notes. "It holds approximately a pint of liquid."

A slender Junoesquian girl appeared on the screen, standing with the jungle at her back. She wore a white cotton dress with tiny blue flowers embroidered on it. Her long black hair hung straight down her back. Leather straps attached to the sandals on her feet and crisscrossed up her calves.

As deep blue as my eyes were, hers ran the opposite spectrum. Their icy color contrasted dramatically with her dark skin and hair. Her eyes held uncertainty, and her slight smile spoke hesitance and shyness.

She was beautiful.

Before joining the Specialists, I'd never paid such close attention to a person's physical details. I'd never searched for answers in their eyes and smile. It was incredible how much I could learn about someone by observing them.

"This is Jaaci," TL explained. "She's the only surviving member of the Muemiraa tribe. She's lived in the Junoesque Jungle her entire life."

I leaned back in my chair. "This is the girl who found the vase?"

"Yes." TL folded his hands on top of the table. "Here's where things get tricky. This vase has popped up here and there throughout history. Roughly a century ago it disappeared, seemingly into thin air. It has been a much sought after artifact. And numerous different tribal nations have it documented as being in their possession at one time or another."

TL nodded toward the screen and the picture of Jaaci. "On her father's death bed, he told her about this vase and where it was hidden. He told her to locate it and, once she did, to pay homage to the Muemiraa gods by finding the ocean and throwing it in to reunite the vase with its creator."

"Find the ocean and throw it in?" I couldn't imagine living in the jungle my entire life and my dying father telling me to find the ocean.

Would that be left or right, Dad?

"I suspect her father knew that if the vase got into the wrong hands, it would be used for evil. The vase is intended to work with nature, not control it." TL stood. "But when she walked from the jungle she strolled straight onto an excavation dig. One thing led to the next, and now the whole world knows about this."

He got up and made his way around the table. "As I mentioned before, the vase is centuries old. Documentation shows fifteen different tribal nations have held the artifact at one time. No one can prove they are the rightful owner, but they all want to be. Legend has it that whoever owns the vase prospers beyond imagination and never suffers again. Here's where the Specialists come in, and here's where I hand things over to Jonathan."

Jonathan?

TL gave the remote to Jonathan, and he stood. "I spent a number of years in the jungles of South America, including the Junoesque Jungle, as a warfare specialist with the IPNC. I know most of it like my childhood backyard. A few of the tribes involved are violent rivals. TL and I have discussed things and have decided I'll be point man on this mission."

TL took his seat. "Jonathan will be in charge. I'll provide assistance from home base, which will give me time to wrap up a few other things and attend some meetings with prospective Specialists' clients."

This would be weird. I'd never been on a mission without TL. I wondered what type of leader Jonathan would be.

He'd gone on the Ushbanian mission as my modeling agent. I smiled a little as I recalled our disguises—me as the spoiled model and he as my boisterous agent. He'd worn a different colored eye patch to match every colorful suit and had buffed his bald head every morning. Other than on that mission, I'd never seen him wear anything other than PT clothes.

Looking at him now, all big and bald, with his black eye patch, I found it hard to conjure up his colorful side. And he'd done it so well.

My gaze drifted to his black eye patch, and I wondered, not for the first time, what had happened to his eye.

Jonathan pressed the remote, bringing my wandering thoughts to attention. Three rows of five pictures each appeared on the screen. All head shots of tribal men. "These are the leaders of the fifteen tribes as they appear in their ceremonial garb. In four weeks they will meet in Rutina, South America, to decide who gets the vase. The North and South American Native Alliance has hired us to provide translation services for the talks and to guard the vase. Each chief is allowed to bring one representative with him from his own tribe."

While Jonathan read off the names of each tribe and its chief, I studied the pictures.

Stern and *proud*. Those two words popped into my head first.

Their ages ranged from forty on up. The oldest one looked to be over ninety. None of them smiled.

Some wore their hair in a long braid, others cropped short, a couple were bald, a few wore traditional head pieces, and one had a Mohawk.

None had beards or mustaches, but some displayed facial tattoos, and others nose or ear piercings.

A man along the bottom row drew my attention more than the others. He had a Mohawk and stripes tattooed down his chin.

It wasn't the Mohawk or even the bold stripes that made him

stand out, although they did add to his uniqueness. It was the look in his eyes. Stern, like the others, but with menace. Like an I-wouldn't-want-to-be-in-a-dark-place-with-him kind of menace.

"The talks will take place on impartial land occupied by the Huworo tribe. They have no documentation that links them to the vase; therefore, their land is considered neutral territory." Jonathan ran his hand over his bald head. "Parrot, this is your first mission. You will go to this meeting as the official translator. There is no technology allowed. As I've already mentioned, each chief will have a personal representative with him. This person knows both English and their chief's native tongue. You, Parrot, will listen to the chiefs speak in their language, translate to English for the personal assistants, and the assistants will translate into their chief's language. There will be ten different dialects and indigenous languages spoken; you are familiar with six. You have four weeks to learn the remaining four."

I blinked. Four weeks to learn four languages? *Holy crap.* Was that even possible?

Parrot cleared his throat. "Sir, can someone else do this? Another agent?"

Jonathan took his seat. "No one has your linguistic brilliance. No one's of Native American descent. Only a Native American translator is allowed at this meeting."

Parrot nodded but showed no expression.

Why wasn't he excited? He was going on his first mission. And not any old mission, either. One that would take him back to his roots, his people.

TL folded his hands on top the table. "Parrot, I know you have a history with one of those men up there." He paused. "So does Jonathan."

Parrot snapped surprised eyes to Jonathan.

"I was there that day. On that Venezuelan runway. I was the guy in the cowboy hat and dark sunglasses." Jonathan adjusted his eye patch. "I spent a good number of years on that case. Because of you, we made significant headway."

Parrot stared at Jonathan, dumbfounded.

What were they talking about?

"Parrot, you're a different person now," David added. "You can do this."

TL cupped Parrot on the shoulder. "You need to put the past behind you."

With a nod, Parrot dropped his gaze to the table.

I stared at his bowed head and the black shininess of his hair. My mind whirled with questions. Which man on the screen was TL referring to? Had something happened between the chief and Parrot? Or maybe Parrot had lived on one of those chief's reservations. Was whatever happened the event that had led the Specialists to him? And what was this about a Venezuelan runway?

And suddenly it occurred to me that every "bad guy" I'd run into so far had had a personal connection with me or one of my teammates.

Some sort of history, a past, plagued every member of my team. None of us came from pristine childhoods. Some had suffered more than others. Could that be one of the reasons why we'd been recruited?

It made me wonder what things I'd yet to learn, or maybe would never learn, about this group.

"GiGi?"

I snapped my attention to TL. "Yes?"

"Did you hear what Jonathan said?"

"No. I'm sorry. I was thinking about the whole situation." TL had talked to me *many* times about my mind-wandering penchant. I hoped he let this one slide.

He cocked a disciplinary brow.

No, guess this one wasn't sliding.

"What can you tell us about cave drawings?" Jonathan repeated himself.

I quickly got my mind back on track. "They're a system of writing where pictorial symbols represent meanings and sounds." Did I sound like a dictionary or what?

Actually, Chapling and I had been working with glyphs for a mission in Egypt that Piper and Curtis, from Team One, were currently on. And I was developing a computer program that translated the ancient writings. "They can be found, surprisingly, everywhere. North America, South America, Europe, Australia . . ."

"I know you've been assisting Chapling with the Egypt mission and decoding some drawings. And he tells me you've taken the initiative to create a translation program. According to him, you've made considerable progress."

I nodded, swelling a bit with pride. It really was a cool program.

"Give us a quick rundown."

I took a moment to simplify things in my brain. "Piper found some glyphs, and she and Curtis were poring through research books trying to figure them out. It made sense to me to code it all into a program that'll do the work for them. This way we can scan in the drawings and my program will provide the various translations. But I'm still in the initial stages." And I had a long way to go. It was a good thing the glyphs weren't a key part of the Egypt mission, because I had weeks and weeks of work to do to perfect the program.

With a nod, Jonathan clicked his pen. "Good. The Junoesquian girl, Jaaci, retrieved the artifact from a cave. A cave that has never been documented in history but has always been a legend. According to her deceased father and the legend, the drawings in the cave are an ancient native code revealing a key piece of information about the vase. Obviously, we don't know what that information is, but we are speculating it will reveal who the vase belongs to. So while Parrot's translating the meetings, you'll be in the cave decoding glyphs with your new program."

"But . . ." I detected a whiny note to my tone and concentrated on sounding more collected. "Why can't we just video feed everything back here so Chapling and I can work on it together?"

Jonathan pushed back from the table. "Sorry. It's against Rutina law to photograph or film the caves. Besides that, a good majority of the glyphs are too faded to show up clearly on film."

My shoulders dropped. Of course they were.

The conference door opened and Chapling, my mentor, waddled in. "Sorry. Sorrysorrysorry. Got sidetracked. Sidetracked sidetracked."

I couldn't help but smile. Chapling had a unique way of bringing that out in me.

Climbing up into the chair beside David, Chapling plunked a folder down on the table. He looked at TL and then Jonathan. "Am I up?"

They both waved him on.

Chapling rubbed his hands together. "Okay. Preliminary intel has revealed the drawings are a combination of numerous cultural glyphs. It would take a historian years to decipher the pattern." He looked across the table at me. "But with smart girl's new program, it can all come together in a matter of days."

Great. Talk about pressure.

Chapling tapped his fingers together. "Which is a good thing because I just intercepted a message between two unknown parties that they are planning on stealing the vase." He slid his folder down the table to Jonathan.

"Meaning," David spoke, "that you've got to decipher the glyphs as soon as possible and find out what the key piece of information is."

I did say pressure, right?

Jonathan stood. "Do your best to find out who those unknown parties are."

Chapling nodded.

"Anything else?"

Chapling shook his head.

Jonathan nodded to TL, who gathered up the folders in front of him. "Okay, follow us," TL said.

He led us from the conference room and down the hall. When we passed my computer lab, Chapling ducked off inside. We crossed in front of Wirenut's electronic warehouse and Beaker's chemistry lab and came to a stop at one of the mysterious locked doors.

When I first came to the Specialists, these secret doors drove me insane with curiosity. After seeing what was behind three of the six, though, I suspected the remaining doors had something to do with Parrot, Mystic, and Bruiser's specialties.

Then again, in this new life of mine I'd learned not to expect the expected. Just when I thought I'd figured something out, it'd turn out different.

TL pointed to the key pad. "This is coded in Uopoei, your first language. For now your code is simply the address of the last place you lived. I want you to change your code within twelve hours and inform me of the new one."

Parrot nodded. "Yes, sir."

TL stepped aside. "This is your room, your work area. You may come here during any free time you have."

Huh. I had only been allowed one hour an evening in my special room. Granted, now I could go anytime I liked, but in the beginning it'd only been an hour. Come to think of it, Wirenut and Beaker hadn't been limited in their time, either.

Parrot punched in his code. The door slid open to reveal an

elevator. This was different. Mine, Wirenut, and Beaker's doors opened directly into our special rooms.

David, TL, Jonathan, Parrot, and I stepped inside the car, and the door slid closed. I glanced around. Nothing unusual. Just a plain old elevator. Except there was no directional panel with numbers and arrows. Instead, a panel of black glass, about one inch wide by six inches long, ran horizontal on the door.

David stepped up and looked into it. A retinal scan. Cool.

"This retinal scan is programmed to read you and me and TL," David explained to Parrot. "You'll stand looking in for three seconds."

The elevator slowly ascended.

Ascended. I *knew* there were floors between the underground conference area and the ranch level. Every day was like a new discovery around this place.

The elevator stopped. David motioned Parrot to do the retinal scan. "This is Subfloor Two."

The door slid open, and I followed the guys out. "If the ranch is ground level and the conference area is Subfloor Four, what's on Sub One and Three?" I asked.

"You'll find out when the time is right," TL answered.

I smiled. I knew TL would say that, but I just had to ask.

We entered a large room approximately fifty by fifty. Flat-screen TVs covered every inch of the four walls. The news silently played on every screen. Countries, dialects, and regions labeled the top of each monitor. Liberia, Australia, the Netherlands, Thailand, and on, and on. Some countries I'd never even heard of.

A control panel, complete with headphones, a keyboard, buttons, and dials, spanned the center of the room. Two white leather chairs sat in front of it.

TL crossed to the center. "Parrot, this is where you'll do your research. Let's say, for example, you're going to Japan." He typed Japan on the keyboard.

All the monitors in front of us tuned in to Japanese television and radio programs.

"This is every single TV and radio station playing in Japan right now. If you want to watch cartoons"—TL picked up a laser remote and pointed the red beam at the cartoon station—"you simply select it."

The flat screens changed channels until Japanese cartoons took up the entire area.

"And for volume"—TL rotated a dial on the control panel—"here's your knob."

Surround-sound Japanese cartoons filled the room.

Neat. Parrot must be ecstatic. I glanced over at him, smiling, excited for him. But his face held no expression as he watched the cartoons.

"You know Japanese." TL muted the cartoons. "Name a language you don't know."

Parrot thought for a second. "There's an island in the South Pacific whose inhabitants speak Loura."

TL keyed in Loura. The screen changed to display different television and radio stations from the South Pacific.

He handed Parrot the remote. "You have five minutes to say

this"—he indicated a paper on the control panel—"in Loura."
TL turned the volume knob.

Oh my God. Was he kidding?

With a calmness that *I* certainly didn't feel, Parrot pointed
the remote. One by one he flipped through the TV and radio
stations.

I watched his concentrated face as he tuned everything out
and focused on the new language, listening, learning.

"Fepqu, bee, aor, hikn . . ." Parrot started trying words a minute later.

Words slowly turned to sentences. Sentences took paragraph
form. Then Parrot picked up the paper and read it.

My jaw dropped. Granted, it wasn't completely seamless,
but certainly better than expected. Unbelievable, in fact. Not
even five minutes had passed. Given more time, he would have
sounded like a true native of that South Pacific island.

"Good, Parrot." Jonathan slapped him on the back. "Beyond
good."

Parrot put the paper down. "Thanks."

I grinned. "Wow."

He spared me a brief smile, and I got the impression he'd
rather be anywhere but here.

TL folded his arms. "I'd like you to tell me what you know
about North and South Native American languages."

Parrot thought for a minute. "I know there're more than
seven hundred Native American languages currently spoken,
with about two hundred here in the States and in Canada, about

seventy in Meso-America, and five hundred in South America. And none of these languages is primitive. Their structure varies greatly. Probably the most characteristic sounds come from the back of the larynx, and a number of vowels are pronounced as nasal sounds. These languages also tend to use just one word to communicate a complex idea. The word order in a sentence is usually subject-object-verb, but subject-verb-object is also used. And many unrelated tribes have similar consonant systems. Most tribes, depending on their locale, have borrowed words from different countries depending on who they've interacted with over the years."

Parrot stopped. "I could go on, but it's pretty boring."

I blinked. Sheesh, he knew his stuff.

TL picked up an earpiece with a slim mike attached. "This is for one-on-one practice with a native speaker." TL checked his watch. "You're scheduled to converse with a Fino native in a few minutes. It's one of the languages you need to learn for your upcoming trip. After that you need to go to bed and get some sleep and start fresh in the morning. I'll let you all know when you'll begin your series of inoculations. And, of course, horseback-riding lessons, as that will be your main mode of transportation."

My stomach dropped. "Inoculations?" Needles weren't exactly a thrilling thought.

"We're going into the jungle," Jonathan said. "We'll be exposed to malaria, yellow fever, typhoid, diphtheria, and rabies, to name just a few."

I cringed. "Exactly how many shots are we talking about?"

"A lot."

I paused for a second as my brain rewound. "Wait a minute, did you say horseback riding?"

"Yes," TL answered.

I waited, but he said nothing else. Did they really expect me to ride a horse? Hello? *Me?* Queen of uncoordination?

TL handed Parrot the earpiece. "I'll leave you to it. Chapling and I will explain the rest of this room to you tomorrow."

"Yes, sir," Parrot responded.

As I followed TL, David, and Jonathan back into the elevator, I glanced back at Parrot. He put the earpiece on and took a seat, looking so sad I wanted to stay and talk or stand silently nearby. Anything to be a friend.

TL stepped up to the retinal scan. "GiGi, Chapling will be expecting you first thing in the morning."

"Yes, sir," I answered, and then it hit me, the things I'd been curious about. Normally I kept my questions in and quietly accepted things. But being with the Specialists had made me more bold.

With a glance at David, I turned to TL. "Sir, I'd like to know the answers to two questions."

He nodded. "Proceed."

"Question number one: Why didn't you take Parrot's monitoring patch? And question number two: How come you gave me only one hour a day in my lab when I first had access to it, yet you put no restrictions on Parrot, Wirenut, or Beaker?" I realized question number two came out like I was accusing TL of picking favorites, but I didn't mean it to. I just wanted to know.

TL folded his arms. "I took Parrot's monitoring patch months ago when we returned from Ushbania."

"Oh." Why hadn't I known? I knew when TL took Wirenut's and Beaker's. Why hadn't TL told me about Parrot?

Because TL doesn't answer to me. I answer to him.

Right.

"Initially," TL continued, "I only gave you one hour because I knew you would become another Chapling if I didn't restrict your time."

I smiled. Chapling lived in the computer lab. He rarely came aboveground. In fact, I'd only seen him up top at the ranch a few times that I could recall.

TL was right. I could *very* easily become another Chapling. TL had seen that tendency in me and made decisions in my best interest. It made me feel all warm and fuzzy that he cared so much.

The elevator opened, and we stepped out. Jonathan headed left toward the front door of the ranch house.

I turned to TL. "Well, thanks for having my back."

"Sure." He chuckled and pointed down the hall. "Now get some sleep. You have a lot of work to do tomorrow. David, come with me."

"Slave driver," I mumbled.

my watch alarm vibrated at 6:00 the next morning. With a low moan, I fumbled in the dark for it on my nightstand and pressed the button that turned off the alarm.

I swung my legs over the side of the bed and sat for a minute with my eyes closed, debating whether or not I could sneak five more minutes of sleep. I rubbed my eyes and convinced myself I'd gotten more rest than the four hours I really had.

With a resolute sigh, I forced my eyelids open and gazed with envy at my roommates, who all snuggled in, snoring away a lazy Sunday morning.

I pushed up from my bed and padded across the carpet to the bathroom. As I passed Cat's bed, I noticed she'd fallen asleep with her earphones in. A slight *chchch* hissed in the air, telling me music was still playing.

Across the room Beaker smacked her lips and rolled over in bed, rousing me from my sleepy trance, and I continued on to the bathroom.

Twenty minutes later, showered and dressed in jeans and a T-shirt, I made my way from our bedroom down the hall to the cafeteria.

Normally food held no significance in my life. I could take it or leave it. But the cook always served bacon with pecan pancakes on Sunday mornings. The combination rocked my world. As I entered the cafeteria, I inhaled the awesome salty/sweet aroma, and a content smile curved my lips.

With its aluminum tables and chairs, our dining hall resembled a miniature version of a school cafeteria. Except the food was much better.

TL sat alone at a table to my right. An empty plate with syrup remnants sat to his left, and the morning newspaper littered the space in front of him.

Mystic stood at the beverage center making a cup of herbal tea. Beside him stretched the buffet piled with food.

"Morning," I greeted TL, eyeing the mound of bacon on the buffet table.

"Good morning." He folded his paper. "Eat lots. I know it's your favorite."

I smiled. It wasn't often he made casual, nonbusiness conversation.

I crossed the dining hall to the buffet and picked up a plate. Mystic stepped up beside me. Forking up three gorgeous pancakes, I glanced over at him. "You're up early."

He sipped his tea. "I'm going to meditate with the sunrise."

"Mmm." Why anyone would voluntarily get up this early stretched beyond my comprehension.

"The fruit's fresh. I recommend the melon."

I moved down the buffet line, bypassing the fruit, and piled on the bacon.

He *tsk*ed me, "Bad girl," and snagged a pecan from my top pancake.

"Hey." I slapped his hand with a piece of bacon.

Mystic laughed. "How can somebody so skinny eat all that food?"

I picked up the syrup bottle and drenched my mountain of breakfast. "Not sure. I think this might weigh more than me."

With another laugh, he headed off. "Later, gator."

TL had gone, and so I ate alone, having no problem devouring and sopping up every last bite.

Fifteen minutes later, as I was dumping my garbage, Parrot walked in.

"Hey." I smiled.

"Hey," he replied, a blank expression on his face.

"Food's good," I tried for conversation.

Nodding, Parrot strode over to the buffet, grabbed a pancake, put some bacon on it, and rolled it up. He took a bite and headed right past me.

"You wanna hang out later?" I called to his back, trying so hard to be a friend.

"Thanks, but I've got a lot to do," he answered, not turning back, and disappeared out the cafeteria door.

I didn't take it personally. That was Parrot. Quiet, contemplative, stoic, a guy of few words. And that was when he was feeling fine. Factor in his obvious discontent with this mission, and I knew he'd be locked up tight.

But . . . that wasn't good enough for me. I unclipped my cell from my waistband and texted him. SORRY. CAN U COME BACK, PLEASE? I HAVE A QUESTION.

I sat back down where I'd eaten breakfast and waited.

A few seconds later he reappeared. "What's up?"

I tried to think of a nonpersonal question to ask, something pertaining to the mission, but came up empty. I wanted to *know* Parrot. I motioned to the seat across from me. "Sit. Let's talk."

Parrot sighed, as if it was the worst thing I could have asked him to do.

"Please?"

Slowly, he approached the table and slid into a chair across from me.

Conversation wasn't my strong point, and it certainly wasn't his. So I knew this wouldn't be the easiest. "We're going on a mission together. I . . . want to get to know you better. And you need to know me. So what do you want to know?" Good. Not a bad tactic. Have him ask me questions first.

"Playing twenty questions, huh?" he tried for humor.

I smiled. "Whatcha got for me? Ask me anything."

"All right. I'll play." He thought for a second. "Where were you born?"

"Right here."

"You mean in California?"

"Yes, California. Right here in San Belden."

He lifted his brows. "No kidding?"

I told him about living at the ranch as a small kid and how David and I had known each other even back then.

Parrot didn't respond for a few seconds. "That's amazing."

I nodded. "I know. And you? Where were you born?"

"Arizona. On a reservation."

"What was it like to live on a reservation?"

He shrugged. "Same as anywhere, I guess. Most people think we live all basic and old-world. It's understandable ignorance. I lived my whole life in an apartment. Went to school. Did my chores. We had traditional stuff, too, just like any culture has. Ceremonies, holidays . . ."

"Did you get to wear any of those cool clothes I've seen in the movies?"

Parrot laughed. "Yeah, traditional clothes when the occasion called for it."

"Favorite color?" I continued with the questions.

Blue for him. Green for me.

"Favorite food?" He asked.

Tacos for him. Lollipops for me.

"Lollipops aren't food," he teased.

"Sure they are," I defended myself, and we laughed again.

Parrot's cell beeped, and he glanced down. "I got to go. I've got another native speaker who I'm scheduled to converse with in my lab."

I nodded, smiling. "I'm glad we had a chance to talk."

He reached across the table and squeezed my arm. "Me, too. I'll see ya later."

"'Bye." I watched him walk from the cafeteria and then made my way to the elevator and down to Subfloor Four.

Keying in my code to the computer lab, I stepped through, and the door suctioned closed behind me.

Chapling stood in the corner, his arms braced on the table that held the coffee, staring at it as if it were a lifeline.

I smiled at the sight. "Hey."

Around a yawn, he glanced up—"Hey"—and went right back to staring at the brewing coffee. "Just got out of bed. Need caffeine. Major caffeine."

"Where exactly *is* your bed?" I asked, realizing I didn't know such a simple thing.

"Right by TL's room."

"You mean that door that's always closed? I'd assumed it was a closet."

Chapling nodded.

"But I never see you come and go."

Looking up, he smiled broadly. "Yes!" He grabbed the coffee and poured the thick muck into his never-been-washed mug, then took a gurgly sip. "Oh, yes. Yesyesyesyesyes." He held his mug up. "Want some?"

I crinkled my nose. "No." I loved coffee, but not Chapling's brand of "mud."

He waddled across the room and flipped a light switch on, off, and back on again. The cement wall behind the switch shifted back an inch and then slid left, revealing a five-foot-tall compartment wide enough to hold one chubby redheaded little person.

I did a double take. What the . . . ?

"It's a tunneling elevator. Goes up and down and side to side. I can go just about anywhere on the ranch in this thing."

"Cool." I crossed the lab to where Chapling stood and crouched down to check out the elevator. "So you go to your room in this?"

He nodded. "Anywhere."

Way back when I first moved into the ranch, I'd been in the barn with TL, Wirenut, David, and Jonathan, prepping for the Ushbanian mission. Chapling had appeared from nowhere, and I'd wondered where he'd come from. "Can you go to the barn in this thing?"

Chapling sipped his coffee. "Yepper."

I stepped back from the tunneling elevator. "I want one."

Giggling, he flipped the light switch again, and the door slid from the left to merge seamlessly back with the wall.

Chapling hobbled over to his computer station and climbed up. "So I hear you and David tore up the Boardwalk last night."

Rolling my chair out, I took a seat. "For someone who never leaves this cave, you sure know a lot."

He cut me a sly glance. "Yes, I do, don't I?"

I narrowed my eyes. "What does that mean? What are you up to?"

Chapling's sly glance transformed into pure childish mischievousness. He took his wireless mouse and, *click, click, click,* then turned his monitor so I could see.

Across his flat screen, small black-and-white video boxes flicked on. I ran my gaze over them, realizing they portrayed every room in the ranch as well as the pool, the barn, and all angles of the outside.

In the top right corner I watched as Mystic sat on the hill behind the house meditating. The video box beside it displayed Bruiser stretched out on her bed, still sleeping. In the bottom left corner, Jonathan jumped rope in the barn. I saw Beaker in the bathroom, brushing her teeth. In the cafeteria, Wirenut and Cat served themselves from the buffet line. TL sat at his desk, studying a file. David pulled a T-shirt over his head, giving me a quick glance of his gorgeous bare chest. Behind David, Adam said something and David cracked up. And there in the middle sat me and Chapling staring at his computer.

I waved at myself, and Chapling giggled.

He clicked the mouse a couple more times and the screens flicked to another scene. The date stamp in the lower right corner read yesterday evening. I glanced through all the video boxes on the screen and zeroed in on me and David making out in the truck.

My face caught on fire. I put my hand in front of the screen. "Chapling!"

He giggled again and clicked everything off.

I laughed with him; I couldn't help it. "You're awful. I had no idea you were such a voyeur. Where are all the cameras?"

"The cameras are hidden everywhere. Lamps, light switches, faucets, pictures, furniture. And I'm not a voyeur. I rarely even look at all this. It's just in case something happens."

I folded my arms and gave him my best disciplinary glare. "Then how come you knew about me and David?"

"Because I updated the video software last night. Your smoochy-smoochy scene was kind of hard to ignore."

I felt my face grow warm again. "Well, anyway . . . we've got work to do."

Chapling saluted me. "You're up."

I rolled my chair back over to my computer station. "Let's talk about the Rutina mission. It's illegal to video or to take pictures of the glyphs. Any ideas on what to do about that? Somehow I've got to get them into my computer so I can work with the symbols."

"Yeah, TL, Jonathan, and I discussed that last night. TL's arranged for a hieroglyphic historian and artist to accompany you all on the mission. This guy works for the IPNC. He'll sketch the graphics, and you can scan them into your laptop. The alliance doesn't know about your new program. They just know there're a couple of historians, you and this guy, coming to analyze the cave drawings and provide a translation of them."

I nodded. "Between his expertise and my new program, we should be able to figure out the code."

On the cart beside me, a stack of hieroglyphic books stood waiting. I'd been through about half of them so far, turning their words and pictures into code for my new translation program.

I was still in the initial stages, and, although I hadn't said anything, I didn't feel confident I could have it ready in two weeks.

There were so many minute details about cave drawings. And the ones in Rutina were a combination of many different cultures. That was one of the main purposes of my program, though. To take patterned, documented glyphs, break them down, be able to decipher combinations of drawings from different cultures, and come up with a highly probable translation. But even if I worked around the clock, I wasn't sure . . . I just wasn't sure.

And what if I couldn't figure them out? What if my new program didn't come through? What would we do? These cave drawings were a key factor in this mission.

My brain stopped its doubtful tirade as I realized this was all stuff I normally argued to TL. He would then assure me I could do it, and I would force myself to succeed. And sure enough in the end, I'd always come through. Kind of weird I hadn't put up an argument with him this time and, in fact, didn't really want him to know I doubted myself. I wanted him to think I felt confident with my abilities.

Hmmm . . . funny how things had changed. How *I* had changed.

Breathing out a rush of focused breath, I grabbed one of the worn, hard leather books and got down to work.

4

MY FINGERS RACED over the keys as I input code into my glyph-translation program. A week had gone by, and I wasn't nearly as close to completing it as I thought I'd be.

"Hey."

One week gone, and only three weeks to go before we left for Rutina, South America.

"Hello?"

I concentrated on the recently scanned glyphs and the measurements I'd taken of them. I referenced the meanings from my research books and merged the two. I ran a quick script to assure they understood each other.

"Yo?"

I compared it to yesterday's rendering, hoping, *hoping*, they worked in conjunction . . . I watched as my screen scrolled with garbled language. Aaarrrggghhh . . . What was I doing wrong?

"*GiGi!*"

I jumped, almost tipping over in my chair.

Chapling stepped into my line of vision. His Brillo-pad hair poofed out into a red Afro as he grinned and waved. "Lunchtime. Go eat."

I narrowed my eyes. "You interrupted me for *that*?"

He showed me a text message on his phone. "Boss man says you have to."

With a groan I rubbed my sore neck. "I have too much work to do to go eat."

Pursing his lips, Chapling leaned forward and checked out my screen. "Want me to take a look?"

"Do you have time?" TL had Chapling working on something that he couldn't tell me about.

He shrugged. "I got time."

"Okay." I'd take any help I could get. Rolling out my chair, I got to my feet.

Chapling took my spot. Climbing up, he studied my screen. Seconds later, he put his chubby fingers on my keys, and they took on a life of their own.

I moved in closer and watched over his shoulder as he wove through my code, quickly making adjustments. He deleted a po-graph formula and added an emblematic cryptogram. He tweaked a cunei theorem and rearranged a subsequence rubric.

Huh, I hadn't thought to do that.

Chapling stopped typing and sat staring at the screen. I waited, my gaze fixed to the monitor, wondering what he'd do next.

He cleared his throat. "You're still here. TL says you have to take at least thirty minutes."

It took a second to realize he was talking to me. "Oh . . . sorry." With a sigh, I turned and set out from the lab, through the underground hallways, and up the elevator to the dining hall.

The place sat empty. A lingering scent of bleach told me everyone had come and gone and the tables had been wiped down. I glanced at my watch, noting it was an hour past the usual lunchtime. On a table to the left sat a few snacks for those who might be hungry in between meals. I grabbed a banana and a granola bar.

As I peeled the skin from the banana, I realized I'd barely seen Parrot in the week since we'd found out about the mission. And most of the times I had seen him, he'd been quiet and had kept to himself.

Taking a bite out of my banana, I left the cafeteria, made my way down the hall to the guys' bedroom, and knocked on the door.

"Yeah?" Wirenut answered. "Come in."

The boys' room looked like a masculine version of the girls' room and always smelled like Mystic's incense. Like ours, their roomy living quarters held enough space for ten more guys. Crème walls and carpet instead of peach-colored. Three twin-size beds with brown comforters in lieu of beige, and a four-drawer, dark wood dresser for each of them replaced the white. A long closet stretched along the left wall where ours spanned the back. A bathroom sat in the back corner with three sinks, showers, and toilets. Posters of skimpily-dressed girls hung from their walls.

Typical.

Wirenut lay sprawled across the carpet writing in a notebook. Green Day played softly in the background. Or at least I assumed it was Green Day because they were Wirenut's favorite.

I never knew the names of bands. Other people knew names of bands. I knew names of . . . well, code.

I sat down on his bed. "What are you doing?"

"Calculus." He cursed and erased something he'd written.

This was the focused, don't-bother-me Wirenut. "I know you're busy, but have you seen Parrot?"

Not looking up, Wirenut shook his head.

Mystic came from the bathroom, wiping his hands on his jeans. "Oh, hey, GiGi. Good thing I wasn't naked."

I smiled. "Good thing."

He pointed to Wirenut. "Unless you want your head bitten off, I highly recommend you go nowhere near him." Mystic went to his dresser and pulled out a pair of socks. "I gave him a citrine crystal, but he refuses to use it."

"A citrine crystal?"

Mystic sat down on his bed and put on his socks. "It unites personal power. Endurance. Helps you mentally focus and control your emotions."

"That sounds handy." I glanced down at Wirenut. "Why won't you use it?"

Wirenut rolled onto his back. "Because its mumbo jumbo." He scrubbed his hands over his face. "Listen, if you're going to be in here, then I'm leaving. Otherwise, you all need to get out of here. I've got hours of homework ahead of me."

"Come on." Mystic grabbed his wallet and headed from the room. "Leave the grouch to his books."

I followed Mystic into the hall. "Where ya going?"

He shoved his wallet down his back pocket. "Please. It's Sunday. Our one and only free day. Where have I gone every Sunday for the past six months?"

I rolled my eyes. "To the Boardwalk to watch the girls Roller-Blade."

Mystic crossed the hall to David's room and knocked. Adam, David's teammate and roommate, opened the door. At six feet five, with blond hair and blue eyes, he and I could easily pass for brother and sister.

"Ready?" asked Mystic.

Adam switched please-tell-me-you're-not-going eyes to me.

I held up my hands. "Boys only."

Bruiser came out of our room and bounded up beside me. "You two going girl watching? Won't be near as much fun today. Have you been outside? It's drizzling. I bet there won't be any bikinis. They'll all be in rain gear."

Adam leaned down nose to nose with Bruiser's five-foot height. She had to love that. She liked him. Big-time.

He waggled his brows. "You'd be surprised what girls wear when they're out and about on a Sunday afternoon in front of a couple hot, eligible men."

Bruiser busted out laughing. "Hot, eligible men? Oh, that's funny."

Smiling, Adam picked her up and set her aside. "Let's go, Mystic."

They made it to the end of the hall. "Hey," I called over Bruiser's gasps for air. "Have either of you seen Parrot?"

Adam and Mystic shook their heads.

"Didn't even sleep in the room last night," Mystic said.

Waving them off, I looked down at Bruiser. "How about you?"

She sniffed and wiped her eyes. "Nope."

I made my way down the hall to TL's office. I peeked inside his open door. "Excuse me. Is Parrot in his language room?"

At his computer, TL didn't stop clicking keys. "No."

"Do you know where he is?"

"Yes."

I waited, but TL didn't expound on his answer. "Can you tell me where?"

TL continued typing. "He's in the barn."

"Okay, thanks."

"GiGi?" TL stopped typing and looked up as I turned around. "This is a hard time for Parrot."

"I know, sir. That's why I'm trying to find him."

I left the ranch house, crossed the wet, grassy yard to the barn, and entered the wide-open doors. The front half served as our physical training area, complete with weights, mats, hanging bags, and other various gymlike stuff.

The back half of the barn served as a . . . well, a barn. Complete with stalls, horses, hay, and gear.

The place always sat deserted on Sundays with everyone enjoying their day off.

A muffled sneeze filtered through the air. Parrot had the worst hay allergies. It always made me smile at the fact that he loved horses yet was allergic to hay.

I strode through the musty training area back to the stalls and peeked over each door. Parrot stood in the second to the last, leaning against the wood wall, idly petting a horse's nose.

"Hey." I propped my arms along the top of the half door.

Parrot glanced over, looking so emotionally and physically tired that I just wanted to rock him to sleep.

He brushed his fingers across the horse's muzzle. "I brought Carrot with me when I came to the Specialists."

By Carrot, I assumed he meant the horse. Sad to say, I didn't know any of the animal's names. "Let me guess, you named him Carrot because he likes carrots."

"No, I named him Carrot because he was orange when I found him."

"Orange?"

He gave the horse a sugar cube. "Some kids had spray painted him as a joke."

"That's not funny."

"No, it wasn't." Parrot stroked the length of Carrot's head. "He's been my best friend for ten years."

How sad.

But then I never even had a best friend, animal or human, until I joined the Specialists.

I picked a piece of hay from the feed bin. "I know you're not looking forward to the trip. Want to talk about it?"

"No, not really." Parrot paused, stroking the horse's ear. "But I want to warn you about somebody."

"Okay."

"There's a chief who'll be there. His name's Talon. He's not a nice man, especially to women." Parrot stopped petting the horse and looked me dead in the eyes. "Be careful. Don't go anywhere near him. I mean it, GiGi."

Parrot's serious tone brought goose bumps to my arms. "What does he look like?"

"Mohawk, stripes tattooed down his chin."

Another chill zinged my skin. "I noticed him out of all the others when we saw the photos of each chief. He looked menacing."

"He's more than menacing. Talon is evil. His soul is dark."

I thought about all the bad guys I'd run into since joining the Specialists. I thought about the different degrees of "darkness" to their personalities and wondered aloud, "What do you think makes a person go bad? Are they born that way? Do they voluntarily become bad? Is it the way they're raised?"

Parrot shrugged. "Talon had a great father. I remember him interacting with us kids on the reservation, playing games or just talking with us. He was a very warm man. Powerful, too. He never made me feel any less for being half Native American. I'll never forget him."

"What happened to him?"

"He died from old age, natural causes. And our customs say that the oldest son steps up and takes over."

"And that was Talon?"

Parrot shook his head. "No, Talon had an older brother. I remember him well. He was just as wonderful as his father. He would have made a great chief."

"*Would* have?"

"After their father died, Talon and his brother went up into the cliffs for prayer." Parrot looked at me. "Talon was the only one who returned."

My eyes widened. "Did Talon kill his brother so he could become chief?"

"That's what everyone on my reservation speculated, but it could never be proven. Talon said his brother slipped and fell off one of the cliffs."

"Oh my God."

"I remember my grandmother told me once that, even as a boy, something was off in Talon. That he always had an evil spirit." Parrot rubbed his horse's ear. "Just listen to me and don't go near him."

"Okay."

Questions spiraled through my brain about Talon and Parrot and their history together. Was Talon the reason Parrot got recruited by the Specialists? What had happened to Parrot's family? Had he been abandoned, orphaned? Was he a runaway?

I studied the side of Parrot's face, wanting to ask him all those questions, but something about his expression told me he wouldn't answer them. Not yet, at least. "Do all those languages stay in your head?" I asked instead.

Parrot grabbed a brush hanging from a nail on the wall, clearly more at ease with the direction of our conversation. "Yeah, sort of. They all hang out in the back of my head waiting for me to call them up."

"Don't you ever get confused? I can barely keep English straight."

"No." He shrugged. "I don't know how to explain it. It's just natural for me, always has been."

"Do you ever forget a language?"

"Sometimes." Parrot stroked the brush down the horse's side. "But all I have to do is hear someone speak it, and I'm good."

"Huh." I twirled the hay I held between my fingers. This language thing fascinated me. "And the new languages? How do you learn them so quickly?"

It took me a whole week to learn five words in Ushbanian. Talk about slow.

He mulled my question around for a few seconds. "I listen for the rhythm, the clicks, the guttural thumps." He chuckled. "That doesn't make any sense to you, does it?"

I laughed with him, pleased to hear his lightened mood. "You're right, it doesn't."

A quiet minute passed as I watched him brush the horse and listened to its heavy breaths.

"Dreams?" I asked. "What language do you dream in?"

"They're silent and black and white, like an old movie."

"That's your brain's way of telling you it needs quiet for a while." I put the hay in my mouth and chewed on the end.

"Think about it. You've got a whole world living in your head. It has to wear out your poor brain."

Parrot smiled. "That's a good way to put it."

"Excuse me, GiGi?"

I glanced over my shoulder. David, my *boyfriend*, stood across the barn in the doorway backlit by a ray of sun that filtered through the cloudy sky. My stomach fluttered. With my preoccupation with my translation program, I'd barely seen him in the past week. And I certainly hadn't gotten any more of his yummy kisses.

"Be right back," I said to Parrot, who smiled and nodded. I jogged across the barn to my *boyfriend* David.

His dark eyes crinkled. "Hey, gorgeous. Long time no see."

"Hey."

David took my hand. "TL's sending me to Egypt to help Piper and Curtis with a few things."

My joy at seeing him drained away. "What?"

"I'm leaving tomorrow morning. I don't know how long I'll be gone. Do you want to go for a walk or something? Just the two of us?"

But I'd be leaving for South America in a few weeks. What if David didn't get back before I left? It'd be forever before we saw each other again. "What are you helping them with?"

He squeezed my hand. "I'm not allowed to say. I'm sorry."

Nodding, I looked down at our joined hands. "It sucks having secrets."

David moved closer. "Yes, it does. But one day we'll both have the clearance to talk freely with each other about our work."

He had more clearance than any of us.

A breeze flowed in, messing my hair. He smoothed the stray strands from my cheek. "So what do you say? Want to go for a walk?"

I glanced back through the barn to the stalls. I didn't want Parrot to be alone. He needed somebody other than his horse, and I wanted him to know he could count on me as a friend.

With a soft smile, I turned to David. "I would *love* to spend time with you. *Believe* me. But Parrot's back there all alone, and I think he needs a friend right now. I'm sorry. Please understand."

Making the right decision, picking Parrot over David, a friend over my boyfriend, brought me peace and a sense of maturity I'd never experienced before.

David kissed my cheek. "Don't apologize. Your dedication to your friends is one of the many reasons I adore you. We'll find each other later."

He slipped something from his back pocket and brought it around. A lollipop! I grinned. He was the greatest guy on the entire planet. He handed it to me and gave me another quick kiss.

"That's forty-one," I said as he stepped away.

He looked at me, clearly not understanding, then it dawned on him, and he smiled. "No, it's thirty-nine."

I watched him stroll away, scrolling my mind through every kiss. I never miscalculated anything. Surely, he'd made a mistake.

Then it hit me, and I giggled silently to myself. I'd included the kisses in my dreams last night.

I'm such a goof.

I made my way back to the stall and peeked over the door again. With his eyes closed, Parrot sat propped against the wall, his legs outstretched in the hay. His horse stood beside him with her head hung low, resting her muzzle on his shoulder.

The tender scene brought a small smile to my face.

"Thanks for staying," Parrot whispered, not opening his eyes.

His heartfelt words flowed through me, settling a content warmth in my soul. I was so glad I'd made the decision I'd made. "You're welcome," I whispered back.

I unlatched the stall door, stepped inside, and relatched. Shuffling across the hay-covered floor, I slid down beside Parrot, linked fingers with him, and laid my head on his shoulder.

Closing my eyes, I listened to his horse breathing. I inhaled the scent of clean hay and absorbed the slight lifting of his shoulder as he breathed.

Time passed, and the three of us stayed like that—Parrot and I quietly bonding and his horse breathing softly on his shoulder.

A few minutes later, Parrot rested his cheek on my head. "I never met my dad."

My heart gave a slow thump, realizing Parrot was about to open up a bit. "No?"

"He died before I was born."

How sad. At least I had *some* memories of mine. "Do you have any pictures of him?"

"Some. I don't look anything like him."

"You look like your mom?"

He lifted his cheek from my head. "My grandmother, actually. Or, at least, what she looked like before she got sick."

"Sick? Is she . . . gone?" Death was never an easy topic to discuss. Most people dodged it altogether. Only someone who had experienced it could truly understand the depth the pain ran.

Parrot nodded. "She was sick a long time. I have no idea what she died of. She refused to go to the doctors."

"Did she raise you?"

Silence.

"I guess that's what you could call it," he cryptically answered.

I imagined if she was sick, Parrot probably raised himself while taking care of her. "And your mom?" I asked.

"I had her until I was seven, and then my grandmother took over, but she was already sick at that point."

"What happened to your mom?"

Seconds ticked by quietly, and, from his silence, I knew the subject of his mom was closest to his heart and most likely off limits.

He laid his cheek back on my head. "I don't know," he said so quietly I almost didn't hear him. "I don't know where she is."

"Is TL trying to find her?"

"Yes."

I squeezed his hand. "Then he will."

With a quiet sigh, Parrot got to his feet. He paced the stall, not looking at me, obviously in deep thought. With each turn of his pace, I detected agitation growing in him. Finally, he shook his head. "I don't know, GiGi, I don't know. He should have found her by now."

"Parrot . . ." Even I knew the difficulties in finding someone.

"With all the technology and the resources around this place. With all the people he knows. He should have found her."

"Parrot . . ." He was getting agitated, a side of him I'd never seen before.

He pointed his finger at me. "And you know what just occurred to me? TL's manipulating me just like Talon did. All everybody wants from me is my language ability, and no one gives me anything in return."

I got to my feet. "That's not true."

"TL's used me for exactly what he wanted, and he hasn't come through with his end of the bargain yet in finding my mother."

"Parrot . . ." I didn't know what to say. I knew exactly how he felt. I'd felt the same way a couple of times.

Parrot kicked some hay across the stall. "I should give him an ultimatum, just like you did. Find my mother or I'm leaving the Specialists."

"You don't want to do that. I made a *huge* mistake when I did that. There are other ways to handle your frustration. And I realize that now because of all the mess I got in with bulldogging my way to Barracuda Key and getting Eduardo." I took a step toward him. "Please listen to me—"

Parrot spun toward me. "I'm *tired* of listening. I'm *tired* of doing what people want. I'm *tired* of not getting what I want."

I put my hand over my heart, feeling his frustration all the way to the core of my soul. "I know what it's like to lose a parent and to do anything for retribution or to get that parent back. Not many people can say they understand what you're feeling, but you *know* I do. All of us here are like you in one way or another. None of us have homes, have families. You don't want to leave. Please, please, *please,* listen to me and believe what TL has told you. He *will* find your mother."

Parrot closed his eyes and dropped his head back. "I just want my life to make sense. I want things, for once, to come together for me."

I closed the small distance between us. "I want the same thing. I want my life to make sense, too. I want to feel settled. I want to feel completed. Being here with all of you is the first time I've felt a smidgen of wholeness." I grabbed his arm. "And I know you feel the same way. Trust that feeling. It's a good thing. It's right. You're meant to be here."

He opened his eyes and looked straight into mine.

"Don't let personal emotions cloud your judgment. It's okay to trust us, your team. We love you." I smiled. "*I* love you. I won't let anything happen to you. Just like I know you won't let anything happen to me."

Parrot stared deep into my eyes, then reached out and pulled me into his arms.

I hugged him hard, hoping he felt my raw honesty. Hoping he made the right decision.

He pulled out of our hug a good solid minute later. "Who

knew you'd turn out to be the resident psychologist?" he said, smiling.

We both chuckled at that.

Parrot nodded. "I'm going to do this mission. And afterward, if TL still hasn't found my mother, well, we'll see."

It wasn't exactly what I had hoped to hear, but it was something. And I understood where Parrot was coming from. Now all I could do was hope that he decided to stay, and I wondered if I could somehow help find his mom.

⠿ ⠿ ⠿

Later that night, I went for a walk. With all the talk about Parrot's family, I was missing my parents a lot. I needed to clear my head. As I made my way out of the ranch into the yard, I found David near the pool. With a three-quarters moon and a clear sky full of stars, it cast a romantic aura over the quiet night.

He lay on a lounge chair staring up at the stars, and as I approached, he lifted his head and smiled.

Holding out his hand, David nodded me toward him, and I crawled onto his lounge chair. Neither one of us spoke a word as we lay side by side, holding hands, staring up at the sky.

Some time later, he pulled me close, and I rested my cheek on his chest.

He let out a long sigh. "I'll miss you," he whispered, and minutes later began breathing heavy.

I listened to him sleep, smiling. I'd miss him, too.

⊞ ⊞ ⊞

ᴏne ᴡeeᴋ ʟaᴛer, ɪ ᴍeᴛ TL and Parrot at the elevator hidden behind the mural. We were scheduled to begin our inoculations.

Nothing like a good needle to start your day out right.

Jonathan walked up. "Everybody ready to get stuck?"

We all smiled.

The elevator opened, and we boarded at the ranch level. TL pulled what looked like a quarter from his pocket and pointed it to the bottom left corner of the car.

Parrot and I exchanged a curious glance. What was going on?

He pressed the center of the quarter, and a yellow laser shot out. "We're going to Subfloor Three."

I perked up. "Subfloor Three?" How cool. "What's on it?"

TL pointed the quarter to the bottom right corner of the car, and a yellow laser shot out again. "Brand-new medical clinic. We just finished it two weeks ago."

How in the world? "You mean people have been down there building a clinic, and none of us knew it?"

"Yes." TL did the quarter-laser thing to the bottom right corner.

I hadn't seen anybody come and go from the ranch. "How did they get down there?" Maybe another secret passageway like Chapling's?

TL did the quarter-laser thing to the final corner and the elevator slowly descended. I waited for him to answer my question, but he didn't.

"TL, did you hear my question?"

TL put the quarter back in his pocket. "Yes. And I'm not answering it."

And there you had it. Yet another secret.

The elevator opened, and we all stepped out into what looked like an empty hospital emergency room. I scanned the area and estimated it to be roughly fifty by fifty feet.

To the right sat three rooms with their doors standing open. I peeked inside and saw, basically, a hospital room with a bed, TV, bathroom, and a couple of chairs. To the left sat three rooms as well. One appeared to be an operating room, the other had equipment in it, and the last mirrored a dentist's exam room.

Along the back wall sat cabinets with medicines, gauze, needles, rubber gloves, and other miscellaneous medical supplies. Beside the cabinets sat a couple of wheelchairs, IV stands, and a crash cart.

"You are looking at a fully functional hospital," TL said. "From now on, for anything we need medically, we go here. And this"—he pointed toward one of the exam rooms—"is Dr. Gretchen."

Parrot and I turned . . . and simultaneously flinched.

Dressed in a white lab coat and taking up the entire doorway stood the biggest woman I had ever seen. She towered at least six feet four inches and probably weighed two hundred and fifty pounds of solid muscle.

With her salt-and-pepper hair pulled back in a tight bun, hands fisted on her hips, and legs spread wide, she scowled back at us.

I swallowed.

She moved her scowl from me, to Parrot, and landed on Jonathan. "Jonathan," she growled in a voice deeper than Jonathan's.

I turned and looked at Jonathan. I swore I saw him swallow uneasily, too. "Been a long time, Gretchen."

She snorted. "I see you're still wearing that eye patch."

Jonathan didn't respond.

Parrot and I exchanged a quick, inquisitive glance.

"Dr. Gretchen has worked for the IPNC for twenty years," TL began the introduction. "She's one of the best doctors I've ever worked with. She and I have been talking over the past several weeks, and I'm incredibly pleased to announce that she's accepted my offer to work for the Specialists as the head of our medical clinic."

I smiled, deciding this was a woman I definitely needed to like me. With my klutziness, there was no telling how often I might be down here. "Nice to meet you, Dr. Gretchen."

She took her eyes off Jonathan and narrowed them in on me. I kept my smile in place.

With a brusque nod in my direction, she tromped across the clinic and over to the cabinets.

In my peripheral vision I saw Jonathan wipe sweat off his

forehead. Interesting. These two obviously knew each other. I wondered what the history was, exactly. Had they been on missions together? Had they trained together? Had they dated?

The last thought almost made me laugh. I couldn't see the two of them together.

Dr. Gretchen pulled out a series of needles and vials. I tried real hard not to look at the size of the needles.

"I'll do the guys," she rasped, "in Exam Room One. And the girl in Exam Room Two."

I didn't bother telling her my name was GiGi, not "girl." I figured that'd come in time.

Carrying a tray with the supplies, she stomped into Exam Room Two, and I followed. "You can do the guys first, if you want." I knew my suggestion wouldn't fly, but I threw it out there anyway.

Dr. Gretchen shut the door. "Drop your pants. Lean over the table. This one's going in the butt."

"Okay." So much for my suggestion.

I dropped my pants and leaned over the table. I saw her reach for a needle and squeezed my eyes shut. I heard her unwrapping something. Then she pulled down my underwear a little, and I felt something wet, presumably alcohol.

I cringed, knowing what came next. I waited, and waited . . .

She smoothed something in place and snapped my underwear up. "All done. See you tomorrow for the next one."

"All done? But . . ." I twisted around and pulled my underwear down, and sure enough there was a bandage. "I didn't feel anything."

Dr. Gretchen got this cocky look. "Of course you didn't. TL said I was the best."

I pulled my pants up. "How big was the needle you used?"

She picked up a clean one from the tray and held it up.

My eyes widened. "That's huge!"

She smirked. "And Jonathan's going to feel every inch of it."

Spinning on her heel, she swung open the door and trudged out. I hurried behind her and watched as she flung open the guys' door. "Drop your pants," she grunted. "This one's going in the butt."

The door closed.

TL stood nearby, leaning against the wall. With a quick glance in his direction, I pressed my ear to the door, wishing beyond wishes that I could be in there to watch.

"You first, little guy," Dr. Gretchen said.

I knew she was referring to Parrot, because Jonathan was in no way little.

A couple of seconds ticked by. "All done," she rasped.

"And now you, Jonathan." I could visualize her getting an evil smirk on her face.

A couple more seconds ticked by . . .

"Ahhh! Ooowww!" Jonathan yelled. "Dammit, Gretchen!"

I put my hand over my mouth to hold in my laugh.

A couple seconds later, the door opened, and Dr. Gretchen nearly floated out with a huge grin on her face. She winked at me and whistled her way across the clinic, then disappeared into another room.

Parrot came out first, obviously trying to hold in a laugh, then Jonathan, holding his butt. Without a look in any of our directions he wiped his eye, stomped over to the elevator, and pressed the button. As soon as the door opened, he stepped inside and jammed his finger on the button. The door closed, and TL broke out in a laugh.

It was the first time I'd ever seen TL do such a thing, and Parrot and I joined in with him.

░ ░ ░

PT. PHYSICAL TRAINING. ROLLED AROUND a few days later. I entered the barn and saw Parrot warming up and headed straight for him. "Hey, you. How's it going in your language lab?"

He smiled a little. "It's a pretty cool setup."

I pulled my hair back in a ponytail. "You going to be ready?"

"Not a problem."

"I wanted to ask you something." I slid a folded piece of paper from my pocket. "I'm inputting some cave drawings from Argentina into my program, and I keep seeing this pattern of words." I handed him the paper. "Does it mean anything to you?"

Parrot studied the rows of letters. A couple of seconds ticked by. "How weird. This is written in both French and Spanish." He pointed to this first word. "First word French, second is Spanish, alternating across the line in that pattern. Drop down to the second line and it switches out. Third line switches again." He handed back the paper. "But that's from the seventeen hundreds. They don't use words like that now."

I folded the paper and slipped it back into my pocket. "I should have come to you days ago." I'd wasted *way* too much time on that one aspect. Sometimes I forgot how valuable my team was. "Thanks."

"No problem."

"All right," Jonathan graveled. "Spread out. Arm's length between you." Jonathan raised his arms to demonstrate, and winced, touching his upper arm where he, Parrot, and I had gotten another vaccine.

I looked at Parrot, and we silently laughed.

Used to the routine, my teammates and I took our spots in the barn/training area and went through our usual stretching drill. It seemed so empty with David, Piper, and Curtis gone to Egypt. And Tina and Adam were meeting with TL about something.

"Okay," Jonathan said about ten minutes later. "Balancing act today." He pointed across the barn to where he'd set up what looked like an obstacle course with balance beams, square tiles suspended by ropes hooked to the roof, and a platform with wheels. "Parrot and GiGi will encounter all types of terrain in the jungle: rivers, trees, bridges, waterfalls, boulders. So we're going to work out the kinks and fine-tune our equilibrium, while I give you some general information about the jungle. Very simply, you are going to traverse these obstacles without falling off. There are mats below you, so don't worry about it if you do fall."

Ugh. Equilibrium was definitely *not* my specialty. Thank God for mats.

"I want the lineup to be," Jonathan continued, "Wirenut, Bruiser, Beaker, Cat, Mystic, Parrot, and GiGi."

I breathed a sigh of relief at being last as we all shuffled across the barn.

Wirenut climbed right up on the balance beam. "Do we get bonus points for theatrics?"

Ignoring Wirenut's humor, Jonathan nodded to the beam. "Anytime you're ready."

Being so agile, I knew Wirenut would do well at this. Bruiser and Cat would, too. It'd be interesting to see how the rest of us would do.

Wirenut danced effortlessly across the balance beam, throwing in a couple of spins for show. He threw his foot out and touched the first floating tile, then the next, and then the next. Ten in all, pretty much sailing across them. He plopped down on the platform supported by wheels, faked like he was going to fall, and, with a silly snort, skipped across it. He did a flip in the air off the end, and then bowed.

We all dutifully laughed and applauded.

"When you're in the jungle, or any other situation for that matter, you have to understand your strengths and weaknesses," Jonathan said. "You can't assume your team member will pick up your slack. You are the only person you can rely on." He nodded to Bruiser. "Go ahead."

She stepped up onto the balance beam and shot Wirenut a

dude-I'm-so-going-to-outdo-you look. Turning around, she did a series of backflips all the way down the beam and off, landing hands down on the first floating tile. She walked across the tile with her hands, keeping her toes pointed in the air, then landed on the wheeled platform in a split. She bounced up, caught air, and sailed off the other end.

I'd seen her in action plenty of times, but her skill level still amazed me.

With a cocky wink to Wirenut, she strutted past him, blowing her nails and buffing them on her shirt.

"The jungle," Jonathan spoke. "There is no other landscape like it in the world. Dense vegetation. Heat, humidity. Steep, mountainous terrain. Rivers. All of these things hinder movement. Restrict visibility." He nodded to Beaker.

She climbed up with no showmanship to her at all. Holding her arms out for balance, she carefully made her way across the beam. Reaching out, she grabbed the ropes supporting the floating tiles and used them to wobble across. She jumped down onto the wheeled platform and stood for a second balancing herself, then crossed it and jumped off.

Not bad. No doubt our cheerleading training for our last mission had helped her.

"If you're in a situation you're not comfortable with," Jonathan said, "stop and think. Ask yourself: What is my objective? What is my terrain? Is there an enemy nearby? Is there a team member nearby? How much time do I have to meet my objective? What resources do I have at my disposal?" He nodded to Cat.

She climbed up and traversed the obstacle course, doing just as well as Wirenut.

Then Mystic, who, of course, had to meditate to channel the balance gods before gracefully completing the course.

Then Parrot, who seemed to perform a little better than Beaker, but not as well as Cat. I was sure his years of horseback riding gave him a natural balancing ability.

"Lastly"—Jonathan looked right at me—"be confident with your movements. The jungle is no place to question yourself." He nodded me to the balance beam.

I walked over, going over everything Jonathan had just said . . . and felt a bit overwhelmed.

With all eyes on me, I stepped up onto the balance beam. So far no one had fallen off. Mystic almost had at the floating tiles and Beaker nearly lost it on the platform, but they'd both managed to recover.

Everyone knew I had exactly zero coordinated bones/muscles/organs/ligaments and whatever else in my body. And I knew, just knew, that they knew I was about to really entertain them.

I glanced over at them all lined up, trying to hide their smiles.

"Whenever you're ready," Jonathan encouraged me.

Taking a deep breath, I pulled my shoulders back, stretched my arms out for balance, and fastened my gaze to the end of the beam. Carefully, I put one foot in front of the other and made it all the way to the end. I turned to my friends with a "take-that" smirk.

"Save that look until *after* the floating tiles," Wirenut teased.

Bruiser snorted.

If I didn't love them so much, I might have had to hate them.

Grasping the ropes supporting the floating tiles, I placed my right foot on the first tile . . . and swung forward . . . then backward . . . and forward . . . then backward . . . The swaying motion made me dizzy, and I squeezed my eyes shut. Both my legs and arms began uncontrollably shaking.

My teammates busted out laughing, and I fell flat on my face on the mat below.

Sigh. At least we had a full-service hospital now. I suspected that Dr. Gretchen and I were going to be fast buddies.

▦ ▦ ▦

A COUPLE OF DAYS LATER I met Jonathan, Parrot, and TL outside the barn. Parrot stood with his horse, Carrot, beside him. And TL had a pretty brown one beside him.

Off to the side was Dr. Gretchen, holding a doctor's bag.

I gave her an inquisitive glance.

With a wink to me, she held up her bag. "Just in case, GiGi."

I smiled weakly. Great. She'd been here only a week and already knew I pretty much needed her on call. Well, at least she addressed me by my name now.

TL held up the reins. "This will be your mode of transportation in the jungle."

"Right," I replied, clearly not looking forward to this.

"Have you ever ridden a horse?" Jonathan asked, turning toward me.

I shook my head. I mean, really, did they even need to ask?

Parrot reached up and stroked his hand down Carrot's muzzle. "Give her a pat."

Cautiously, I approached and reached my hand out to touch her muzzle.

Carrot snorted and jerked her head away.

I took a quick step back. "This isn't going to work." Clearly they were going to have to think of another way to transport me through the jungle.

"It's obvious you're scared," Parrot said. "She's picking up on it. Don't let her see that you're intimidated. Take charge. Be confident. Be sure of your movements. You're the boss."

"Easier said than done." I took a fortifying breath and stepped toward her again. Quickly, with what I thought was confidence, I gave her a pat. Carrot just stood there and let me do it.

Cool.

Parrot walked around her, trailing his hand over her body. "Now this. Let her get used to your movements."

Following Parrot, I strolled around her, gliding my hand over her back and sides. Again, she just stood there and let me do it.

Not bad.

"Now mounting." TL grabbed hold of the saddle. "Watch." Standing on his horse's left side, he grabbed the saddle horn, placed his left boot in the stirrup, and effortlessly jumped up and swung his right leg over. "Now you try." He nodded to Carrot.

Parrot stepped back to give me room. I circled around her again, letting her feel my touch. I figured that would be the smart thing to do. Grabbing on to the saddle horn, I hoisted my left tennis shoe into the stirrup. With a grunt I pulled myself up . . . and slid right back down.

Carrot sidestepped away, and I one-foot hopped to keep up. "Whoa, girl, whoa." I glanced up at her, and she slanted me a haughty look.

"Did you all see that?" I jabbed my finger at the horse. "She gave me a look."

Parrot laughed. "She did not give you a look. She's picking up on your body language. Don't hesitate at all. Walk up, put your foot in the stirrup, and go right up into the saddle."

Walk up, put my foot in the stirrup, and go right up into the saddle? I almost snorted. That takes coordination, and coordination definitely did not exist in my repertoire of gifts.

"Don't just pull up either," Jonathan advised. "Use your leg muscle to push at the same time you're pulling."

"Shouldn't one of you be helping me?" Especially since they all sounded like such experts.

"You need to do this on your own," Jonathan commented.

I looked at Parrot, and he nodded his agreement.

I didn't know why I had to do this on my own. Probably had something to do with me and Carrot bonding. My new BFF. Blah, blah, blah.

Taking another fortifying breath, I stepped up to her side. I grabbed the saddle, wedged my foot in the stirrup, and pushed/pulled myself up.

My leg swung over, and I found myself sitting astride Carrot.

She turned her head and winked at me, and I blinked. Now that definitely had to have been my imagination. Horses couldn't wink, could they?

"She's proud of you," Parrot said.

"She is?"

Parrot nodded. "Definitely."

I swelled a bit with pride.

"Okay, now use the reins to tell her what you expect." TL walked his horse forward. Gently, he tugged the reins to the right, and his horse followed his lead. Then he demonstrated the same technique going left.

Looked easy enough. Wedging my right boot in the stirrup, I took hold of the reins. Carrot didn't move.

"Um, go?"

"Give her a gentle tap with your heels," Parrot instructed.

I did, and she moved.

Grinning like a goof, I carefully tugged the reins to the right, and she followed my lead. I went left next, and she followed.

Quite pleased with this, I stroked my hand down Carrot's neck. "*You* are the most beautiful, bestess horsey in the world."

Parrot chuckled.

Who would've thought riding a horse would bring me so much joy. No wonder Parrot loved it so much.

TL swung off his horse. "Now let's have you try this horse."

"What? Why can't I stay on her?" I nearly whined.

"Because you need to be exposed to different horses."

"TL's right," Parrot agreed. "Just because Carrot likes you doesn't mean all horses will. You have to get used to different personalities and learn to adjust your body language to fit each horse."

Reluctantly, I dismounted and made my way over to the other horse. I reached my hand out for a pet, and he snorted and reared up.

With a sigh, I stepped back. This was not going to go well.

░ ░ ░

A WEEK LATER I WALKED into the conference room for our last meeting before the mission. We left for South America in one day, and I still had a few tweaks here and there to make on my translation program.

Jonathan sat at one end of the long metal conference table, and TL sat at the other. Parrot had already taken the seat to the left of TL, so I rolled the one out to his right, David's usual spot. I smiled to myself as I sat and swore I detected a hint of David's cologne.

Pushing back from the table, Jonathan stood. At our first mission briefing, I'd wondered what kind of leader he'd be. So far he'd proven to be just as confident and organized as TL.

"Parrot," Jonathan began. "How are things on your end? TL

tells me you've been in your language lab working hard. We leave tomorrow. Are you prepared?"

Parrot nodded. "Yes, sir."

"Parrot's been ready since last week," TL chimed in. "He's more than prepared. He's going to do fine."

Since last week? That meant he learned four languages in three weeks. Jeez. Talk about amazing.

"Tell us what you've been doing in your language lab," Jonathan prompted.

"Well, every day I start out by watching an hour's worth of programming from the different regions that will be represented at the talks. I follow that up with one-on-one conversations over the telephone with the actual assistants who will be attending the talks with the chiefs, not only to get to know them personally, but for a real flavor of their dialect. I've been listening to recordings of the tribes themselves, the women, the children, the everyday activities. And I've been meeting via video conferencing with different historians, learning about the customs of the indigenous people I'll be dealing with." Parrot smiled a little. "I have to say, it's a pretty darn cool lab."

I smiled.

Jonathan turned to me. "And your program, GiGi? All set?"

"Yes," I lied, then immediately felt guilty. "Well, I have a few tweaks, and then, yes, it'll be ready. I need to cross-reference the cave drawings in Rutina with known, documented glyphs and come up with a translation."

I didn't mention the fact that I really didn't feel confident about my program. They wouldn't understand. And if they did, they'd just tell me everything would be fine.

TL clicked his pen. "She'll do fine."

See?

Jonathan referenced his folder. "As you know, we've been hired by the North and South American Native Alliance to provide translation services with both language and the cave drawings. We've also been hired to guard the vase. So in other words, they know we're the Specialists, former government employees who now work privately providing highly skilled services. But they don't know our real identities."

Parrot raised his hand. "But you know I know one of the chiefs. *He* knows my true identity."

"We realize that," TL answered. "Which is why you'll go in disguise. You'll be meeting with a makeup artist tonight to be outfitted."

"Parrot," Jonathan continued, "will go under the name Flint Dunham. GiGi will be Hannah Flowers, and I'll be going as Shane Young."

Oooh, I liked Hannah Flowers. It had a sort of country-girl quality to it.

Jonathan looked first at me and then Parrot. "The talks are scheduled to go for one week. As you all know, Chapling intercepted a message that two unknown parties are planning to steal the vase. More intel has revealed that these two unknown parties are chiefs who will be attending the talks. At this point we do not know which two chiefs they are, but Chapling is continuing to research that.

"This mission is going to be a bit different from others in the past in that we're stepping back in time. This is a ceremonial tribal gathering, free of modern-day conveniences. The men sleep in one area and the women in another. The cave is approximately one mile from the village. The talks will take place in a ceremonial hut located in the center of the village. We'll arrive and depart via horseback. The glyph historian has been there for a week getting a jump-start on things. Our contact will meet us at the airport to take us into the jungle. We'll sleep, eat, and wash outside."

Bathe outside? Wait a minute. . . .

"GiGi"—Jonathan nodded to me—"cultural differences between men and women are very strict. Our contact in Rutina has informed us that Jaaci will be your hostess. It's important that you do exactly what she does."

"But wouldn't it make sense that one of the Huworo women would be my hostess since they're hosting the talks?"

He shook his head. "Only married women in the Huworo tribe are allowed to host. And they're only allowed to host Native Americans. Since you're nonnative, Jaaci has been taken in by the Huworo and given the job."

I didn't know if I liked the fact I'd been deemed a "job."

"Chapling," Jonathan continued, "has installed updated satellite chips in our phones. However, being so deep in the jungle, there will probably be noncommunicative spots. We'll have to figure that out when we get there. Other than our cells and GiGi's laptop, which have been pre-approved by the Alliance, we're taking no technologies with us."

I nearly pouted. No technology? That meant no cool gadgets or neat gizmos. What a bummer. At least I'd have my laptop, my own private version of the Swiss army knife. Only Chapling and I knew the cool things it was capable of.

"The alliance," Jonathan went on, looking at me, "does not know about your new program. Please remember that it's top secret. They think you're there as an assistant to the glyph historian, who will be joining us from the IPNC."

I nodded my understanding.

"Let me stress a few things. The Mother Nature vase is, like TL originally said, a highly coveted item. You are to trust *no one*. A lot of people want this vase, and I'm sure, if properly motivated, they would stop at nothing to get it. Let me remind you that a few of these tribes are long-standing rivals. I'm fully expecting some sort of altercation. Should anything happen to me, you both know how to get ahold of TL. Like he said, he'll be here at home base handling meetings and wrapping up important details."

Should anything happen to me. That statement brought goose bumps to my skin and reminded me of the dangerous, life-threatening situations we were in while on missions.

"Questions?" Jonathan asked.

Parrot and I shook our heads.

"We pull out at oh-seven-hundred hours." Jonathan closed his file. "Dismissed."

5

EARLY THE NEXT morning we boarded our plane. I tucked my laptop under the seat in front of me, and about five minutes later, my cell vibrated. I checked the display.

BREATHE. I'M THINKING OF U.

I smiled at my *boyfriend's* message. David was on a top secret mission and yet risked a security breach just to reassure me.

I had been in a plane crash when I was six, the same one that killed my parents. It didn't take a genius to figure out why I hated flying so much.

I'd learned to tolerate it, though. I had no choice. It came with being a Specialist. Travel was inevitable, and this flight marked my seventh one. Not bad for a girl who was inconsolable the first time around. David had been there that first time, telling me to breathe. Somehow just thinking of him always made the trip go smoother.

I texted him back. I'M BREATHING AND THINKING OF U 2.

I put my cell phone away and turned to Parrot. "How are you?"

He yawned. "Tired. After the farewell party, I wasn't able to sleep."

I lowered our shade and handed him the pillow wedged between my seat and the wall. "Try to sleep now. We have a long week ahead of us."

Through another yawn, he nodded, put the pillow behind his head, and closed his eyes. Just as our plane took off, I heard him inhale a soft snore. It made me smile.

Hours later, in the late afternoon, our plane touched down in Maires, the capital city of Rutina.

Jonathan, Parrot, and I departed the plane into muggy brightness.

"¡Hola!" A small man with a bushy kinky beard called from the other side of the security fence. I assumed he was our local contact.

Jonathan hitched his chin. "Hola, Guillermo. ¿Cómo estás?"

"Bien. Bien."

Jonathan hadn't said if Guillermo was an IPNC agent or not. Since the Specialists used to be a division of the IPNC, and because we were so small, TL still used IPNC agents for freelance work, like this.

We grabbed our duffels and backpacks from the luggage trolley and made our way across the steamy tarmac.

Couples, families, and singles bustled along with us, finding their luggage, talking on cell phones, heading toward the security gate.

The airport stood off to the left. Jonathan had explained that only certain airlines accessed the terminals and everyone else used the outdoors.

Too bad we weren't one of the "lucky airlines."

We joined the long line to security check, and, while the sun baked us, we waited our turn.

Men in military fatigues wandered the crowd, holding machine guns in front of them. Dark shades hid their eyes, and their faces wore matching scowls.

All around us everyone spoke Spanish. The more I listened to the rapid-fire rolling r's, the more I wanted to know what they said.

The woman in front of me laughed at something her friend said, and they both glanced back at me.

"What did they say?" I whispered to Parrot.

He smiled. "Tell you later."

It couldn't be that bad if he was smiling . . . through his mustache. His disguise was too cool. The makeup artist had lightened his hair to brown and woven in extensions, making it fall straight to his shoulders. He wore blue contacts that seemed so real, even if you looked close, you couldn't see the rims of them. He had a mustache and beard trimmed neatly to his face. And randomly placed moles on his forehead, neck, chest, and arms. The moles wouldn't come off unless a specific solution was used to take them off.

Shifting, I peered over everyone's heads (being tall had its advantages) to the security gate, and sighed. We still had at least sixty people in front of us.

Sheesh, you'd think they'd have more than one security check.

Using my shoulder, I wiped sweat from my cheek and fanta-
sized about an icy soda. I repositioned the strap on my laptop case
to crisscross over my body and tried to ignore the heat. Maybe if I
ran code, my brain would be too sidetracked to think about it.

    <&8#2x02 6I4s6o01 |+2!9)3@8|>

    <2&09x#2 #8(3$7*4 =i18n>

    <%</p> (rfc2616) :w3.gro>

Raised voices brought me from my temporary reprise. I focused on the military men pushing through the crowd, not caring
if they shoved a woman, child, or man aside.

I turned to Jonathan. "What's going on?"

He barely shook his head in response.

They yanked a blond woman from the line, and my gut
clenched. I watched wide-eyed as they dragged her kicking,
clawing, and screaming to an awaiting van.

Her echoing wails brought cold prickles to my skin.

Was this actually happening? Out here in the open? And why
wasn't anybody doing anything?

I glanced around. Nobody even looked in the frantic woman's
direction. I turned to Jonathan.

He death-gripped my arm a split second before a military man
yanked me in the opposite direction.

Jonathan held tight to me as the guard barked something in
Spanish.

Jonathan calmly responded.

The guard gripped my other arm and barked the order again.

Jonathan calmly responded.

The guard gave another yank on my arm, and I grimaced and tried to move closer to Jonathan.

He didn't move, but he seemed to grow in size as he pulled back his shoulders, accentuating his already straight posture, solid muscles, and towering height.

The guard didn't let go of me, but it occurred to me then how small he was next to Jonathan. I'd say the guard stood about five foot eight. Shorter than me even.

Jonathan slowly and deliberately enunciated his Spanish, not so calmly now, more threatening and serious.

The guard switched his narrowed dark eyes to me and then beyond me to Parrot.

I swallowed.

Letting go of my arm, the guard stepped to the side. He jabbed his machine gun in the direction of the security shack and snapped out an order in Spanish.

Still holding on to me, Jonathan gave a little tug. "Get your backpack. Let's go." He glanced over his shoulder and motioned with his head for Parrot to follow.

Leaning down, I swung my oversize backpack over my shoulder. "What's going on?" I whispered.

"Not sure. Be quiet and let me do all the talking."

Not a problem, seeing as how I didn't know the language.

The heat from the asphalt seeped up through my flip-flops as we crossed the tarmac.

Jonathan eased his hold on my bicep, and my muscles immediately pulsed with the release of pressure.

I glanced down at my forearm, where the guard had yanked, and saw deep red stripes. I'd probably bruise.

Another man stood guard at the security shack's door. He shifted his gun and gave the metal door two hard whacks. The sound of his fist connecting with metal vibrated in the air around me.

The door opened and a guard dressed just like the others appeared. Both men nonchalantly pointed their machine guns in our direction, telling us in their silent, threatening terms not to try anything.

Jonathan's hold on my bicep tightened again as he led me through the door. Cigarette smoke and air-conditioning overpowered the small, dim interior, bringing goose bumps to my sweaty body.

To the right, a small window let sunshine filter in. In the back left corner a metal desk sat catty-cornered. A man in a suit sat behind that desk, with another guard standing to his side. Newspaper clippings and wanted posters littered the walls.

The guard who had let us in closed the door and moved into position to block the exit. With his feet spread wide, he held the gun diagonally across his body. He grunted something in Spanish, and Parrot looked at Jonathan. Jonathan nodded once, and Parrot moved away from us to stand by the window.

The guard beside the man in the suit stepped out from behind the desk and came straight at me. I resisted the urge to back up as he approached.

Before I had time to blink, he yanked my backpack off my shoulder, and I sucked in a breath. He grabbed hold of my laptop strap, and I ducked before he yanked that and dislocated my shoulder. Luckily, my ducking at the same time he yanked slid the laptop right over my head without injury.

He tossed my stuff against the wall, and I watched in horror as my laptop bounced against the cement.

"Don't say anything," Jonathan ordered, handing over his duffel bag and indicating Parrot to do the same.

The guard tossed their stuff on top of mine. Briskly he patted down Parrot, Jonathan, and me. Then he shoved Jonathan and me toward the desk. Behind me, I heard a zipper as the guard began rifling through our things.

The man in the suit slowly rose to his feet. His serious brown eyes surveyed me from top to bottom and back up. He picked a cigarette from an ashtray and took a long drag and exhaled, squinting at me through the smoke.

Holding back a cough, I quietly cleared my throat as the man continued to scrutinize me.

What was going on? I wanted more than anything to look at Jonathan, but kept my gaze steady with the man in the suit.

He stubbed his cigarette out and continued studying me as he slowly ran his fingers back and forth across his bristled chin.

He said something to me in Spanish.

"I'm sorry. I don't speak your language."

He let out an annoyed sigh and switched his attention to Jonathan. The two of them began a rapid-fire discussion. Back and forth they spoke, and the more they spoke the more agitated the suited man became.

He slammed his fist down, and I jumped. Jonathan didn't even move. The man jabbed his finger at scattered papers, bringing my attention to his desk and upside-down color sketches of a woman.

I tilted my head slightly, trying to make out the drawings.

Jonathan and the suited man continued their argument as I studied the sketches. Something about the woman seemed familiar.

The phone rattled, and the suited man yanked the receiver from its cradle. As he talked, he turned one of the drawings around so we could see it.

The woman had blond hair and light either blue or green eyes. The large shape of the eyes, the thick upper lashes, and the defiant, alert look flashed my brain back to Barracuda Key. My last mission.

A female agent had interceded when I'd confronted Eduardo Villanueva, the man who killed my parents. The female agent's face had been hidden behind a hood, but those eyes . . . something had seemed familiar.

I stared at the picture, itching to pick it up. This woman had the same eyes. My focus switched as I took in her whole face and my gaze touched each of her features.

These policemen thought I was this woman, probably because of the blond hair and eye color. But to me it was obvious I was not.

I glanced over at Jonathan to find him staring at the picture as well. I wanted more than anything to ask him if he knew that woman, but doubted he'd tell me if he did.

Fastening my attention back on the sketch, I decided the woman was probably in her late twenties or early thirties. Was it a recent drawing, I wondered, or an old one?

A list of aliases headlined the sketch and beneath it her crimes. The crimes were written in Spanish, though, so I focused in on the alias names.

Yetta Blomqvist, Wandella Dacey, Fabiene Uarov, Sabine Hiordano . . . on and on I read the names, all from different nationalities. I almost laughed when I got to the last one, Oki Li Ming. The woman in the sketch was most definitely not Asian. I scanned the names again, but none of them rang a bell.

The man in the suit slammed the phone down, jolting me back to attention.

He snapped a hand out and barked an order to Jonathan.

Jonathan glanced over his shoulder to Parrot and nodded, reached inside his back pocket, then said to me, "Give them your passport."

Unsnapping the side pocket on my cargo pants, I slid my passport out and handed it over.

Behind me, the guard who'd been searching our luggage said something. I glanced over my shoulder to see my backpack wide open, with extra computer batteries, bras, underwear, clothes, and toiletries scattered. I nearly groaned at the sight, not only because my box of tampons was on display, but because it had taken me *forever* to get everything packed.

Then I saw my laptop opened and powered up, and my jaw clenched. No one touched my laptop without asking. *No one.*

The guard repeated what he'd said, and I just looked at him.

"Give him your password," Jonathan translated.

"What?!"

"Do it," Jonathan emphasized.

For a couple of seconds I didn't say anything. *Calm down, GiGi, calm down.* Other than Chapling, no one knew how to infiltrate my computer. Different passwords led to different levels of my computer. To any regular person they would find only standard software packages.

"BBCGMPW," I gave him my first-level password, the first initials of my teammates and me. Beaker, Bruiser, Cat, GiGi, Mystic, Parrot, and Wirenut. Just thinking of them helped to calm me down.

Jonathan repeated the letters in Spanish, and the guard typed them in. While he waited for my screen to appear, he pulled a folder from Jonathan's backpack and brought it to the suited man.

I watched as the man rifled through the file. It contained documentation that we had been hired by the North and South Native American Alliance. Proof that we were who we said we were.

Shoving the folder closed, the suited man yanked a piece of

paper from a desk drawer. He slammed the blank paper down in front of me and put a pen on top. *"Escribe tu nombre cinco veces."*

"Write your name five times," Jonathan translated.

Normally I wrote with my right hand. But TL taught all of us to use the opposite hand when on a mission. I had to admit, I'd gotten quite good at writing with my left hand.

Hannah Flowers, I scrawled my fake name five times.

The man in the suit tore the paper away and with a hard jaw he studied the signatures, comparing them to my passport.

I felt a smile tug at my mouth, suddenly amused by his mannerisms. Snapping, yanking, banging, and barking. I wanted to tell him that if he were more in control, like Jonathan or TL always were, his point would come across more effectively. The suited man was angry, we all got it. And I bet he was really upset none of us was acting intimidated.

He looked up at me then, and his eyes narrowed. *"¿De qué te estás sonriendo?"* he shouted.

"He wants to know what you're smiling at," Jonathan repeated, and I swore I heard a hint of amusement in his voice.

I flattened my mouth and dropped my head. *"Lo siento.* I'm sorry." I did know how to say that in their language. Plus, I figured the whole dropped-head, submissive thing would make him feel authoritative and not press the issue.

He grunted and walked from behind the desk across the room to the door. I heard him open it and start speaking to the guard posted outside.

With my head still dropped, I looked at the sketch of the woman again. I quietly but quickly reached out, snagged it, and slid it from the desk. I didn't know who this woman was, but I wanted to know. Especially with the similarities to the agent in Barracuda Key who had taken Eduardo.

Carefully, and very rapidly, I folded the drawing into a small square.

"Front of pants," Jonathan barely whispered.

Head still bowed and body held very still, I tucked the sketch down the front of my cargos, wedging it in the elastic of my underwear.

Seconds later the door closed, and the suited man came to stand back behind the desk.

I turned my head a fraction to the right, and moving only my eyes, I peeked at the guard who'd been searching our things.

He was busy clicking through my laptop looking at random files. Many of them fake, serving as decoys in case something like this ever happened.

The man in the suit took his seat behind the desk. I smelled more than heard him light up another cigarette.

Lifting my head, I brought my eyes up to meet his.

He leaned back in his creaky chair and propped his heels on the edge of the desk. Closing his eyes he took a long drag, and then blew it out through his nose.

What a nasty habit.

At least thirty minutes ticked by as Jonathan, Parrot, and I stood there in silence and the suited man continued smoking. I wanted to remind him that secondhand smoke was just as harmful as if we were smoking ourselves. But, of course, I kept my opinion to myself.

The guard finally finished searching our things and came back to his original position standing next to the suited man.

The phone rattled, and everyone in the room except Jonathan jolted.

The man in the suit picked it up, said a few things, and then listened. *"Gracias."* He hung up the phone. "You are free to leave." He dismissed us using perfect English.

I was astonished. He could speak English? I should've suspected. One of the main things I'd learned in the Specialists was that people were never what they seemed.

Following Jonathan's lead, Parrot and I quickly crammed our belongings into our backpacks and duffels and quietly shuffled from the shack.

Bright heat hit us in a wave as we stepped outside. I took a deep, clean breath, welcoming the muggy warm reprieve from the smoky air-conditioned room.

Beside me Parrot did the same.

I glanced at my watch. We'd been in there for over an hour. *Time flies when you're having fun.* I rolled my eyes at my own stupid humor.

"Don't say anything," Jonathan instructed, quickly leading us toward the gate.

Guillermo, the man who'd greeted us when we first arrived, still stood on the other side of the fence.

A guard with a machine gun opened the chain-link gate and motioned us through.

Silently we filed past. And continuing not to speak, we followed Guillermo through a gravel parking lot, zigzagging around vehicles.

We came to a stop at an old green Land Rover with a rusted white top. It had a tire mounted on its hood, a steel rack on top, and a ladder climbing up the back. A shovel, pick, and hatchet were strapped to the white top. The vehicle looked well used, uncomfortable, and in dire need of a bath.

Guillermo turned the knob on the back window, and it popped up. Jonathan tossed his duffel in, grabbed my backpack and did the same, then signaled for Parrot.

"Climb in," Jonathan told us.

Taking my laptop off, I handed it to Jonathan and climbed up through the window. Jonathan gave me my computer, and I crawled across our stuff he'd tossed in. Two padded benches sat facing each other. I took the one on the left. Parrot climbed in and took the bench across from me. Jonathan closed and latched the back window, cutting off our meager fresh air.

Through the muddy side glass I watched as he and Guillermo came down the side of the vehicle to the front. Guillermo climbed behind the wheel while Jonathan hopped into the passenger side. Guillermo cranked the diesel engine, grinded it into gear, and drove off.

Jonathan slid open the rectangular window that connected the front to the back. "If you guys need air, open the sides."

Parrot and I moved at once, winding open the side windows to let in a stream of humid air. Guillermo and Jonathan opened their windows and began a conversation in Spanish.

I looked at Parrot.

"They're talking about what happened in the guard shack," he translated.

"So Guillermo's one of us?" I whispered to Parrot.

"I'm with the IPNC," Guillermo answered.

"Oh. Sorry." I didn't know why I'd apologized. But it embarrassed me Guillermo had heard my whisper. I should've just asked him straight on.

Guillermo drove us from the airport and onto a two-lane highway.

Parrot pushed out what sounded like a stressed breath.

"You okay?" I asked.

"GiGi, I was really scared back there."

I smiled a little at his admission. "I know—me, too."

"You've been on a lot of missions. Does that kind of stuff happen all the time?"

I thought back to being kidnapped in Ushbania, thrown in a dungeon in Rissala, and coming face-to-face with my parents' killer. "Yes." And strangely enough, I didn't feel nearly as shaken up as usual.

I mean, I'd actually been amused at the gruff manner of the man in the suit. If that would have happened on my first mission, I would have been a nervous wreck. It made me feel a bit evolved, for lack of a better word. Like I was finally getting the hang of this new life of mine.

Parrot didn't say anything else, and so I turned to the world outside. I tried to take in some scenery, but the muddy windows made it nearly impossible.

Sometime later we exited the highway onto a dirt road. Parrot and I gripped our benches as the Land Rover bumped down the road.

"You doing okay?" Parrot asked.

I smiled at the sweet question. "Yeah, I'm okay. You?"

Parrot shrugged. "I'll survive."

I reached across the small distance and squeezed his knee. "Remember I'm here for you. I'm a great listener. And I'm excellent at keeping secrets. If you ever want to talk . . ."

"Thanks." He looked away, and I took that as my cue he was done with the topic.

The Land Rover hit a pothole, jolting me, and I felt the sketch scratch my bare skin. "Oh!" I reached inside the front of my cargos and pulled it out. Gingerly, I unfolded the sweaty drawing, praying the wetness wouldn't tear it. I needed to get it scanned and into my laptop before it was damaged.

I blew on it, trying to dry it a bit.

Using his T-shirt, Parrot dried his sweaty face. "Hey, pretty slick. I didn't know you took that."

I smiled at his surprise.

"Can I see it?" Parrot asked.

I handed it over. "Careful, it's wet."

Gingerly, he took it, cradling it in his hands.

Pulling the rubber band from my limp ponytail, I smoothed my damp hair and redid it. "What does it say below the picture?"

He studied it, balancing it in his hands as the Land Rover bumped down the road. "She's wanted for arson, wire fraud, assault, larceny, burglary, stalking, conspiracy, robbery, drug manufacturing, embezzlement, perjury, extortion, murder, forgery, money laundering, manslaughter, kidnapping . . ."

On and on he read, and when he finally finished, I simply blinked. "Is that even possible? For one person to commit all those crimes?"

With a shrug, he handed the paper back. "I don't know what to tell you."

"Just because it says it on paper doesn't mean it's true," Jonathan commented through the window. He nodded to the sketch. "Get that scanned into your computer as soon as you can. I want to know who that woman is."

"Yes, sir." He'd read my mind.

Then the Land Rover jerked to a stop, and the drawing tore in half.

6

I stared at the moist, frayed edges of the torn picture, and my heart sank. The tear zigzagged through one eye, down the nose, and slashed across the mouth. Key features that any identification program would need to make a match to this sketch.

I should've never gotten it out and opened it up. Especially in a bumpy vehicle. For a genius I could be real stupid sometimes. Now I may never know who this woman was.

Parrot reached across and touched my shoulder. "We'll fix it, GiGi. We'll fix it. I'll help you."

Giving Parrot a tiny smile I really didn't feel, I pulled a folder from my laptop case and opened it up. I slid two pieces of paper out, carefully laid the sketch between them, and tucked the papers back inside the folder. With a sigh, I put it back inside my laptop case and zipped it up. Why did I always make such stupid mistakes?

Guillermo rolled up his window and shoved open his door. "Okay, this is it," he said, interrupting my disappointment. "We go the rest of the way on horseback."

Jonathan rolled up his window, too. "Close up back there."

Parrot and I wound the side glass shut while Guillermo popped open the back hatch and began unloading our things.

I climbed out first and came to an abrupt stop.

I looked around and saw green. Everywhere. In every shade imaginable. Huge, gigantic leaves, some as big as me. Weird plants like nothing I'd ever seen. And trees—my head dropped back as I followed one all the way up—trees as big as skyscrapers.

I turned a slow circle—I couldn't see anything but green. I couldn't even tell where the Land Rover had come from. It appeared as if the foliage had immediately covered our tracks.

And—I straightened a bit—the jungle seemed to pulse and grow right in front of me as it closed us in.

I shut my eyes and gave my head a quick shake.

"I'd recommend you change your shoes," Guillermo suggested, nodding down at my flip-flops.

I completely agreed. Flip-flops and trekking through a jungle were two things that obviously did not go together.

Kneeling beside my backpack, I dug through the disorderliness the guard had left and found a pair of socks and what I affectionately referred to as my kick-butt boots. TL had given each of us a pair.

Very military, with steel toes and thick heels, the black boots laced halfway up my calves. Parrot already wore his, so I sat on the Land Rover's bumper and tied mine on.

"This way," Guillermo said as he stepped through a humongous bush.

"Be back in a minute." Jonathan threw his bag over his shoulder before disappearing into the same pumped-up greenery.

I finished with my boots and zipped my backpack closed.

Jonathan reappeared first, with Guillermo close behind, each with two horses in tow.

Parrot caught sight of the animals and breathed a sigh, as if just looking at them brought him comfort. With a slight smile, he stepped right up.

"Hey, beautiful," he cooed, stroking the muzzle. "I bet you're about five years old." He ran his hand across the horse's neck and down the length of its body.

The brown horse huffed and twitched as Parrot crossed in front of it and trailed his hands along its other side. "You like that, do you?" He laughed.

The brown horse huffed and twitched some more, and I smiled. "I think she has a crush on you."

"The feeling's mutual." Parrot grabbed hold of the horse's mane and effortlessly swung himself up, like he was climbing onto a tricycle instead of a huge animal.

He looked up at Guillermo. "Sorry, I didn't ask. May I ride her? What's her name?"

"Her name's Abrienda. And, yes, you can ride her. I don't think she'd like it too much if I separated you anyway."

Parrot leaned down and nuzzled her ear. "Did you hear that? It's you and me, Abrienda."

My smile got bigger. I couldn't help it. This was the happiest, most content I'd seen Parrot in a long time.

Jonathan handed Parrot his backpack, and Parrot strapped it to the horse's saddle. Guillermo and Jonathan fastened the rest of the duffels and backpacks to the saddles, shoved their feet into the stirrups, and swung themselves up. Leaving me still sitting on the Land Rover's bumper.

All three guys looked down at me.

I checked out Guillermo's pretty white horse, Jonathan's friendly speckled one, Parrot's gentle brown one, and then I looked at mine . . . and swallowed.

Shiny and black, mine stood large and fierce. It might have been my imagination, but he seemed *a lot* bigger than the other horses. Like leader-of-the-pack kind of big.

The horse didn't move as he proudly stared back at me. And I swore his eyes narrowed with dark mischievousness. It was as if he was thinking, *Ah, Blondie's scared of me. That's good. That's reeaally good.*

Nice horsey.

"He's friendly," Guillermo unconvincingly reassured me.

Uh-huh. Sure. "Maybe if I knew his name."

"Diablo," Guillermo answered.

I eyed the horse. "Diablo. Does that mean something?"

"Satan," Parrot said, trying to hide his amusement.

Great. Shouldn't that tell everybody something? Hello? The horse's name is Satan. That couldn't be good. "Can't I ride double with one of you?"

Guillermo shook his head. "Sorry, the trail's too treacherous for double. Diablo's used to strangers. And he's used to the jungle. He knows where's he's going. You'll hardly have to do anything at all."

Jonathan's saddle squeaked as he repositioned himself. "Take your laptop off and strap it to the carabiners on the saddle. It'll give you more balance when you mount."

Recalling my brief horse-riding training, I pretended to be confident as I walked around Diablo, running my hand over his body, letting him feel my touch. I took my laptop case and hooked it to the saddle. I wedged my left boot into his stirrup, grabbed hold of the saddle, and swung right on up. I couldn't help but sigh with relief.

Diablo growled, making his lips vibrate with the rush of air.

I stiffened a little with the sound.

Guillermo walked his horse past the Land Rover. "It'll take us two hours to get there. It'll be dark by then. Everybody stay close. You do *not* want to get lost in the jungle at night."

Jonathan nodded for Parrot and me to follow Guillermo. "I'm bringing up the rear," he said.

We left the small clearing, and our Land Rover, behind and disappeared into the jungle.

In silence we rode in single file, spending most of our time tucked close to our horses to avoid the low-lying branches and vines.

Ducked down on Diablo, I tried to take in some scenery, but my crouched position made it impossible. I ended up resting my hands and cheek on the saddle horn, and for a span of time I stared off to the right watching green Goliath-like leaves, plants, and trees go by.

At some point along the way, I yawned and closed my eyes and melted into the rocking motion of Diablo's steady gait. . . .

I dreamed of David smiling, his eyes doing that sexy crinkling thing as he looked back at me. Of his linking pinkies with me, warmly whispering something into my ear. I dreamed of burying my nose in his neck and slowly breathing in his unique David scent. Of—

"GiGi."

—kissing me, nuzzling my neck—

"GiGi."

I jerked straight up in the saddle.

"You need to stay awake," Jonathan warned. "Look to your left."

Rubbing my eye, I looked to the left . . . and froze.

We were on a cliff.

And it dropped straight down.

Hundreds, *thousands* of feet down. I couldn't even see the bottom.

Not moving a muscle in my body, I stared at the ledge we were on. Each time one of Diablo's hoofs came down, pebbles skidded over the edge and disappeared into God knows where.

With my heart galloping, I inched my head to the right . . . and froze.

Another drop-off.

A really, really, *really* big drop-off.

"J-J-Jonathan?"

"Calm down, GiGi. Diablo knows what he's doing. Concentrate on not moving. Don't do anything to set him off balance."

Locking every muscle in my body, I stared hard at the black hairs of Diablo's mane. I concentrated on not moving, not breathing. I heard a short, choppy, shallow intake of air and realized it was me. In my peripheral vision, the ledge inched by as Diablo *clop-clopped* along, following Guillermo's horse.

Squeezing my eyes shut, I forced a swallow, trying to moisten my mouth. I kept my eyes squeezed shut. I'd rather see darkness than the reality of the minuscule ledge and the vast jungle around me.

I heard another choppy breath come in and out of my mouth and then a deafening roar. "Wh-what was that?!"

7

"IT'S A WATERFALL, GiGi," Jonathan calmly responded. "Relax. You don't want to spook Diablo with your tenseness. Concentrate on unlocking your muscles. You're stiff as a board."

"That's because there is a HUGE dropoff on both sides and a TINY ledge supporting us and a NIAGARA-like waterfall."

"But it's easier on the horse if you move with him. Just relax."

With my eyes still closed, I drew a long breath in through my nose and blew it out slowly through my mouth. *Calm down, GiGi. Jonathan's right. You need to relax. For Diablo's sake and everyone's safety.*

Again, in through my nose and out through my mouth.

But . . . IT WASN'T WORKING!

With a gust of air, Diablo shook his head and took a few steps back.

"Calm. Down," Jonathan gritted through clenched teeth.

"I'm trying!" I hissed back.

My horse took more steps back, forcing Parrot's horse to back up, too.

"GiGi," Parrot snapped. "Please. Calm. Down."

And then I did the only thing I could think of. I recited code, this time out loud.

"*<A ferh=78hic>*

"*<!TNEMELE (led|sni)>*

"*<(%wofl)*>*"

Somewhere in my subconscious, I registered Diablo calming down a little.

"*<%i17m %x16n>*"

Continuing to mumble code, I concentrated on my muscles, flexing, releasing, leaving them loose. I straightened my back and said another string of code, focusing on Diablo's movements and allowing my body to feel them.

"*<deru [DK] gasi {LP}>*"

"Good, GiGi, good," I heard Jonathan say.

I opened my eyes and looked somewhat casually at Guillermo's back as he rode in front of me. I glanced at the ledge stretched in front of him. It was definitely as small as my imagination had made it out to be. We had only about twenty feet to go before we were back on an expanse of jungle ground.

"*<MNB / asd / POI />*"

To my left a waterfall poured from the side of a cliff, gushing through holes in the rock. It roared like an animal as water shot out and dropped into the eternal bliss.

As comfortable as I now felt, I didn't look down. I didn't kid myself that I'd be indifferent to the drop-off. Instead, I concentrated on watching the waterfall, moving with my horse's stride, and reciting more code.

Moments later Diablo left the ledge and stepped onto a cleared area of the jungle. I peeked over my shoulder to see Parrot and Jonathan leave the ledge as well. I glanced beyond Jonathan, and my jaw dropped. The skinny ledge stretched a good solid mile between the two jungles. I couldn't believe I'd just come across that.

Parrot moved his horse up beside mine. "You okay?"

I nodded. "Wow."

He swiped sweat from his face. "No kidding."

"Were you nervous?"

Parrot gave me an incredulous look, and I laughed.

"Seems Diablo is just as much of a nerd as you are," Parrot teased. "Who would have thought code would calm him?"

I gave Diablo's neck a pat. "Nerds unite."

Parrot pointed over his shoulder through the thick overgrowth to where the sun was setting. "It'll be dark soon."

I nodded.

We rode in silence side by side across a clearing that, as soon as we passed through it, closed in to surround us with foliage. My thoughts drifted to what had gone on today: the sketch of the woman, the plane ride, security . . . "Hey, Parrot, what did those girls say in front of us at the security checkpoint?"

Parrot shrugged. "It's nothing. Don't worry about it."

Yeah, right. "Tell me."

"Really, it's nothing."

"*Tell* me."

Parrot sighed. "They thought you and Jonathan were, ya know, together."

"*What?*" I laughed. "But he's *old*."

"They . . . thought he was your sugar daddy."

I coughed. "My *what?*"

"Your sugar daddy. Ya know, one of those men who—"

"I know what a sugar daddy is. Oh my *God*. That's gross."

We both laughed, and I realized how nice it was to have a momentary reprieve from the tension of this mission to just enjoy each other's humor.

"Single it up," Guillermo directed us as the foliage closed in tighter around us. "We have only about five miles left. And we're not outfitted for camping, so keep up."

Parrot took his spot behind me, and we continued our safari through the Junoesque. The sun soon disappeared, and darkness settled in around us. The farther into the jungle's thick overgrowth we trekked, the blacker it became.

I'd never known darkness like this. I couldn't see Guillermo in front of me or even my horse, Diablo, for that matter. I felt, not saw, the foliage around me, brushing my arms and legs and occasionally slapping my face.

If not for Guillermo, Parrot, Jonathan, and, of course, Diablo, I would've been out of my mind in fear of what might have been out there in the inky night.

As if on cue, the jungle suddenly became alive with sound.

Click-clacks. Snaps. Croaks. High-pitched wails. A deafening hiss and hum. It came in stereo from all directions. A symphony of bugs, an orchestra of nocturnal animals. It was the craziest, most all-encompassing sound I'd ever experienced.

Overwhelmed with the energy and overpowering sounds, I hunched down close to Diablo and pressed my fingers to my ears. "Is this normal?" I nearly shouted.

"Yes," Guillermo shouted back.

And then suddenly I felt them, biting my neck, my forearms, my ears, and any exposed skin they could get to. "They're attacking me!" I yelled.

In the darkness I fumbled for my backpack and unzipped the front. I dug out my bug repellant and started spraying it on me, in the air, on Diablo. It helped. A little.

I shoveled blindly through my backpack and found the one and only jacket I'd packed. Frantically, I shoved my arms into it and zipped it up. I'd roast in this heat and humidity, but at least my arms would be covered from the bugs.

Ahead of me Guillermo lit a lamp, and immediately it cast light around us. I sucked in a breath at the sight.

Bugs. Everywhere.

Big ones. Small ones. All colors.

Like something out of a sci-fi movie.

Again I began spraying the air with bug repellant. The insects merely flew through the fog as if it gave them a renewed strength.

Guillermo stopped his horse.

"What are you doing?" I sprayed a red one coming right at me. "We need to gallop through this stuff."

"It'll be like this the whole rest of the way," Guillermo called over the sound.

"What?!" Was he kidding?

Guillermo dismounted from his horse, slid a machete from his saddle, walked over to a tree, and sliced a tumorlike growth from the side of the trunk. He scooped up a handful of tiny squirming bugs, rubbed them together in his hands, then smeared brown liquid guts on his neck, arms, face, and through his hair and bushy beard.

Ew! "What *is* that?"

"Termites." He scooped a handful and brought it to me.

I shook my head. "No, no, no, no, no." Termite guts were going nowhere near my skin.

With a shrug, he continued on to Parrot, who immediately took the bugs, squished them, and began rubbing the goo on himself. Jonathan did the same. I cringed as I watched them, feeling a little sick to my stomach.

Something sharp sank into my exposed neck. I swatted it and felt the same sharpness on my cheek, then my thumb, then my wrist. Screw this. Bring on the termite guts. "Okay, I'll take some!" I yelled almost desperately.

Guillermo brought me a handful of squirming termites, and I didn't stop to think. I took them, rubbed them between my hands, and began spreading the gut liquid on my exposed skin. I didn't even want to *think* of what I must look like.

Within seconds, the bugs flew right past me. Like I had an invisible force field around me. "What about the horses?"

Guillermo climbed back up in his saddle. "They'll be fine. These bugs don't like their blood."

I surveyed Diablo's body, and sure enough he stood bug-free.

"And the village we're going to?" I asked. "Are we going to have to wear termite goop there, too?"

"They burn special spices that ward off the bugs," Guillermo answered.

Oh, thank God.

Guillermo gave his horse a gentle nudge, and we were on our way again. The small lamp he carried gave us a dim yellow glow to navigate by. And as the minutes ticked by, I became used to the jungle's nighttime opera.

No one spoke as we rode along. No one *could* speak with the noise. The darkness seemed to get even darker, if that were possible. Seconds ticked into minutes and at least another hour went by. When *would* we be there? Hadn't Guillermo said it would be only a couple of hours way back at the Land Rover?

"How much longer?" Parrot called through the night.

I smiled as that question brought a sudden memory of my parents to my mind. I'd been five, and my parents and I were in a car. Dad was driving, and Mom was in the passenger seat. I didn't remember where we were going, but I was restless and couldn't wait to get there.

"How much longer?" I'd whined with excitement.

"'Bout another fifteen minutes," my dad replied.

Fifteen minutes went by.

"How much longer?" I asked again, fidgeting with my seat belt.

"'Bout another fifteen minutes," my dad replied.

And on it went, fifteen minutes going by, me asking my dad, and my dad answering the same way. We probably drove for hours having that exact conversation. My dad had either been incredibly patient or truly enjoying my excited misery.

I sighed through my smile, enjoying the bone-deep warmth that came with a memory of my parents. I reached down and rubbed Diablo, just needing some contact and touch.

A flashing flame in the distance brought my attention back to the present. I squinted and made out a few lights scattered through the thick foliage. I kept my eyes peeled to the flickering glow as we drew closer. I saw some sort of hut come into view, and then another, and another.

Diablo followed Guillermo and his horse through a maze of enormous plants, and then we stepped into a clearing. And it was like stepping back into another century.

Fires surrounded by stone barriers flickered throughout the village in no particular order. A large circular-shaped thatched-roof hut occupied the center of the clearing. So large I estimated it could hold approximately fifty people. Tall, flaming torches marked the north, south, east, and west corners of the hut. Smaller, triangular-shaped huts dotted the landscape around the larger one, and a few square ones scattered the area as well.

Although I couldn't see well through the dim light put off by the fires and torches, it appeared as if each hut had a small gar-den in the back.

An opening on each of those triangular dwellings signified its entrance. Other than that, there were no openings in the straw structures. The square ones, however, had no walls at all, only thatched roofs. At such a late hour, it stood to reason the place sat quiet and still. Everyone was probably asleep.

A movement off to the left drew my attention, and I watched as a dark-haired man walked straight across the clearing without a glance in our direction. With his neatly combed hair, kha-ki pants, white shirt, and boots, he looked to be in his early twenties. Maybe a college student? An open book in hand, completely oblivious to his surroundings, he pushed his metal-rimmed glasses up as he read and continued marching across the village.

I almost laughed. I hadn't expected to see a studious little nerd reading a book in the middle of a jungle.

Guillermo urged his horse forward, and we followed. Silently, the four of us filed into the nighttime clearing. Diablo did his vibrating-lip, gush-of-air-out-of-his-mouth thing, and the sound ricocheted through the night.

The nerd jerked at the intrusion and whipped around. His book went one way and his glasses the other. He stood there for a second in shock, staring at us coming toward him. I realized then what we must look like, soaked through from sweat and the hu-midity, with dried brown termite guts all over our skin and hair I'd probably run screaming in the opposite direction if I saw us.

The nerd gave his head a quick shake, and I watched with amusement as he scrambled to pick up his book and glasses. He blew the dust from his lenses and slipped them on, then went back to staring at us.

His mannerisms reminded me . . . of me.

Huh.

Guillermo brought his horse to a stop right in front of the nerd and said something in Spanish.

"I'm sorry. I don't speak Spanish," the nerd responded.

Yep, definitely reminded me of me.

"My name is Guillermo. This is Hannah," he introduced, nodding to me, "Flint, and Shane. We're here for the talks."

The nerd's face brightened. "Oh! Right! Right!" He pushed his glasses up his nose. "I'm Professor Quirk. I'm the resident expert on the cave drawings."

I blinked. "*You're* the professor?" I'd imagined him a *lot* older. "But you're so young."

Professor Quirk looked right at me. "And your purpose here is . . . ?" he asked with a bit of playfulness to his tone.

"I'm here as your quote/unquote assistant. I'm the computer specialist."

"*You're* the computer specialist?" He blinked. "But you're so young."

I narrowed my eyes. "Touché."

Behind his wire-rimmed glasses, he imitated my narrowed eyes.

So this was the guy I'd be holed up with in a cave for the next week. I wonder how *that's* going to go.

Professor Quirk pointed to the other side of the clearing. "You can corral your horses over there." He directed our attention to the triangular-shaped huts bordering the left side of the clearing. "Those first two are for single men." Then he indicated the ones bordering the right of the clearing. "First two over here are for single women. All the other huts are for the families. This big one in the middle is the ceremonial one. It's where the talks will take place."

Guillermo nodded. "Thanks."

"No problem. See you all tomorrow." With that, Professor Quirk turned and continued on his path.

Guillermo led the way through the clearing toward the other side where some horses stood corralled. As we passed the huts, I peeked into the openings but saw only darkness inside. I wished there was another girl with me so I wouldn't have to go into the "single-women" hut by myself. At least Parrot had Jonathan and Guillermo.

We came to a stop at the corral, and all three guys swung their legs over the saddle and effortlessly slid from their horses. I pulled my boots from the stirrups, lifted my right leg to swing it over the saddle, and instantaneously felt a cramp. "Ohhh."

Grimacing, I dragged my leg the rest of the way over the saddle and plunked down to the dirt. My legs immediately began to spasm. "Oh, my God." I grabbed my thigh and massaged it.

The guys unhooked our bags from the horses. They took the saddles and harnesses off. They lined up all the gear along the corral and led the horses inside the gate. They did all this while I continued crouching, massaging my legs. How they could move, I had no idea. One of them might have to carry me to my hut.

Parrot grabbed my stuff and came over to me. "Walk it off. You'll feel a lot better in a minute."

As Guillermo led my horse away, I took my first steps, gritting my teeth at the ache.

A few seconds into my hobbling, Parrot came to an abrupt stop. I glanced up at him first, and then followed his line of sight across the clearing.

There in the doorway of the huge center hut, lit by one of the torches, stood a beefy man with a Mohawk and a tattooed chin. His face held hardness, his eyes stoic darkness.

"Talon," Parrot whispered.

Through The Darkness

I stared at Talon as he looked back at us. In the past year I'd been with the Specialists I'd seen some real scary bad guys. Talon stood short and squatty, and even from the distance I saw the evil in him. This was one man not to mess with.

Standing beside me, Parrot made no move. I could almost feel the fear vibrating off him.

Jonathan stepped up behind us. "You're in disguise," he reminded Parrot. "Talon has no idea who you are."

Parrot barely nodded his comprehension.

Guillermo strode past us. "Come on. Let's call it a night."

Carrying our duffel bags and backpacks, we made our way through the village, crossing to the side of Talon, who still stood in the entryway to the big circular hut. In my peripheral vision, I saw Parrot keep his vision glued to the ground. I chanced a glance at Talon and saw him staring right at Parrot.

Was it possible he recognized him?

No way. I barely even recognized him.

We came to a stop at the first triangular-shaped hut, one of the two that Professor Quirk designated as the "single-men" hut. Guillermo crouched to step inside.

"Wait." I stopped him. "What about me?" Weren't they going to walk me to my hut? Granted, it sat right on the other side of the clearing, but still.

Guillermo glanced up. "Sorry. Single men aren't allowed to go near the single-women huts after nightfall. You'll be fine." With that, he disappeared into the straw structure.

Single men couldn't go near single women? What was this, the 1800s?

I turned to Jonathan, hoping he'd have something better to say.

He merely nodded. "Guillermo's right. You'll be fine."

"B-but how do I know which hut?" Were they kidding me? This was ridiculous.

"Professor Quirk said the first two are designated for single women," Jonathan said.

"Yes. Still, what do I do? Do I look inside of one and if it's packed go to the next one? Do I find an empty spot on the ground inside? Is there a cot? A hammock? My God, am I going to get a blanket? *A sheet?* What if there's nothing nowhere? Do I sleep outside? What about wild animals? Should I find some more of that termite stuff? What if—"

Jonathan put his hand on my shoulder, much like TL did when I slipped into one of my hysterical, neurotic moments. "Calm. Down. You. Will. Be. Fine." Carefully Jonathan enunci-ated each word, probably so they could sink into my overloaded brain. "Peek your head inside the first hut. If you don't see a place to sleep, then go to the second hut. There will be a bed for you in one or the other, I promise. It may be a hammock. It may be a blanket on the floor. I don't know, but there will be something. I promise."

He gave my shoulder a little shake. "Did you understand everything I said?"

I blew out a shaky breath, knowing I was acting ridiculous. "Yes."

"Good. We'll see you in the morning." Jonathan ducked into the single-men hut, leaving me alone with Parrot.

He had to be tied up in knots, yet I was the one freaking over a stupid hut. "How are you?" I asked, reaching for him.

Parrot didn't respond to my touch. With a face void of emotion, he nodded across the clearing. "Go ahead. I'll stand here and make sure you're okay."

"Do you want to tal—"

"Go ahead," he interrupted me, making it more than obvious he didn't want to talk.

With a sigh, I turned and made my way through the darkness across the clearing to the single-women huts. Halfway there, I glanced over my shoulder to make sure Parrot still stood there. Sure enough, he did. As much as I absolutely adored him, this moment made me appreciate him even more. This was all I needed. Someone to watch me and make sure I would be okay. He'd recognized that.

David would've recognized that, too.

I reached the first hut and ducked inside. It took a few seconds for my pupils to adjust to the dark. In the dimness I made out hammocks hanging randomly throughout the space. Squinting my eyes, I ran my gaze over each sleeping hammock occupant and located an empty one in the back.

I peeked my head back out the opening, exchanged an "I'm okay" wave with Parrot, and then meandered through the sleeping bodies to the back.

I didn't bother changing or cleaning up at all—I was thoroughly exhausted. I just dropped my things, climbed into the hammock, and stretched out. I lay there, staring up at the thatched roof, idly listening to the heavy breaths and soft snores of the other women.

I inhaled deeply and picked up a woodsy-spicy smell. I willed myself to sleep, but thoughts of the day occupied my mind. The jungle, horseback riding, bugs, Guillermo, the Land Rover, security, the sketch . . . Who was that woman? I felt confident she and the agent I had spoken to on my last mission were one and the same. But who was that agent?

I rolled over in my hammock, closed my eyes, and my mind drifted to David. . . . I wished so much he was here.

▦ ▦ ▦

A GENTLE TOUCH TO MY shoulder made my eyes flutter open. A girl about my age stood above me, softly smiling down. I blinked a few times before focusing in on her olive skin, shiny straight black hair, and unique light blue eyes.

"You're Jaaci," I said, realizing she was the Junoesquean girl who had walked from the jungle carrying the Mother Nature vase. She was the whole reason we were here.

Nodding, she took a step back, and I swung my legs over the side of the hammock. I took a second to look around the hut now that daylight had come.

Bamboo poles had been tied together and used as supports for the thatch walls and ceiling. Bushels of fruit and vegetables hung on ropes from the bamboo poles. Seeing the bananas made my stomach growl.

Rough, splintery boards lined the walls. Personal items had been placed on them, things like clothes, small boxes, bowls with jewelry, blankets, baskets with beads, and strips of cloth.

As I watched, a half dozen tribal women busied themselves unhooking hammocks, rolling them, and storing them on the boards next to the other personal items. The women were all dressed the same, in colorful, lightweight, knee-length dresses with leather sandals. They all had black hair worn in a long braid. Some wore jewelry, some had bright tattoos on their ankles or wrists, and most looked to be in their teens or early twenties.

"Axw xaqu xe foxlu," Jaaci said.

I scrunched my face. "Do you speak English, by any chance?"

Jaaci shook her head and shrugged, obviously having no idea what I'd asked.

She held out a small a box containing a bar of soap, a rag, and a comb. *"Foxlu."*

"Bath," I understood. "Yes, definitely." I touched my crusty termite-gut hair, then ran my tongue over my unbrushed teeth. *Ugh*. Definitely time to bathe.

Like I'd seen the other women do, I unclipped and rolled my hammock and stowed it on one of the rough wood planks.

I rifled around in my backpack and found soap, a toothbrush, a comb, and a change of clothes. At the bottom of my backpack lay my little stuffed giraffe, the one David had won for me on our date. Just seeing it brought a smile to my face.

I followed all the other girls out into the early morning. Awesome-smelling food assaulted my senses, and I inhaled deeply. I realized that I hadn't eaten since lunch yesterday.

In the daylight, I took in the village. No one was up and around but us girls. All the other huts sat quiet. I checked my watch, calculated the time change, and suddenly felt groggy. Five in the morning? Were they kidding me? It was inhumane to be up at this hour. No wonder nobody else was up and around.

With a sweet smile, Jaaci nodded me in the direction the other girls were walking. We left the clearing and entered the jungle.

Minutes later we stepped onto the bank of a wide, softly rolling river. The girls began taking off their dresses and stepping naked into the water. I stood for a second, stunned, unable to completely wrap my brain around the fact that a bunch of girls were getting naked, out in the open, and stepping into a river. To bathe, nonetheless. And absolutely unselfconsciously, at that.

None of them paid me one single mind as they took their rags and soap and washed. They didn't even look at each other. Obviously, this was something they did together every day.

This must be the single women's time to bathe, I realized, noticing no one else around.

"Axw enob," Jaaci called, waving me into the water.

Well, I could stand here and remain clothed and filthy or get over my hangups, strip, and be clean. I ran my tongue over my teeth again, remembered the crusty termite guts, and opted to get clean.

I fought the urge to cover myself with my hands and tried to act as if I did this every day. Stark white next to their brown bodies, I stepped into the slightly chilly river, my foot slipped on a mossy rock, and I slapped down on my butt.

Inwardly, I groaned. Of all the times for my klutziness to come out, it had to be when I was stepping naked into a river. Leave it to me to make the grand entrance.

A few of the girls glanced quizzically in my direction and then went right back to bathing. A few others let out harmless, good-natured laughs. And a few others just stared at me. *What? Haven't you seen a blond-haired naked white girl sprawled across the rocks before?*

No. Come to think of it, they most likely hadn't.

As soon as I could, I slipped into the water to hide myself and sort of swished my arms and legs around. I glanced down into the water and could make out everything to my knees. Below that, though, my legs disappeared into murkiness. "There aren't any weird fish in here, are there? Piranhas?"

A few of the girls gave me that same quizzical look, and I sighed. I wished someone around here spoke English.

"Weos?" Jaaci held out a brown bar of soap and a rag.

I sighed through a smile, realizing I'd left my soap onshore, and took hers. "Thanks. My name's Hannah, by the way." I pointed to my chest. "Hannah."

"Ha-na," Jaaci tried.

I nodded.

Seeing as how most of the girls had finished and were getting dressed, I began scrubbing my body as quickly as I could. I didn't want to be the only girl left in the water.

A whistling in the distance had me glancing around. That couldn't be a wild animal.

The whistling got a little closer. The pitched vibrations sounded like something from an opera. If that was a wild animal, it certainly had talent.

The sound came closer, and I narrowed in on a spot of jungle about twenty feet in front of me. From the overgrown foliage stepped Professor Quirk.

He wore the same clothes as last night, only wrinkled and untucked. His hair stood on end, his glasses were foggy, and he hadn't shaved. He'd either been up all night or fallen asleep in his clothes and hadn't bothered to clean up yet.

Segueing into a new song, he flipped a page in the book he held and continued reading. As he neared the river he briefly glanced up, then stepped onto a rock that protruded from the water. He stepped on another rock and then another, slowly making his way across the river, still reading his book.

Halfway across he stopped and slowly turned in our direction, obviously realizing there were a bunch of naked girls bathing and dressing. Through his foggy glasses, he stood very still and stared at us.

I crouched real low in the water to the point where only my head stuck out. Even then, I knew I had to be a beacon next to all the other girls. None of them seemed to even notice Professor Quirk standing on a river rock in the distance, staring at us.

I opened my mouth to shout for him to leave, but something made me stop. I studied his dazed stance and realized . . . he didn't even see us. Chapling looked exactly like that when he got lost in thought. And I knew from experience that when I got wrapped up into code, the entire world disappeared into nothing.

Professor Quirk reached behind his glasses and rubbed his eyes before turning back to his book and continuing on across the river.

I finished scrubbing away the termite guts and stood thigh deep scrubbing my hair.

"*Jyyzf,*" Jaaci said.

I opened my eyes and turned around. "What?"

She pointed to my backside. "*Jyyzf.*"

Twisting, I looked behind me. Something black and slimy was attached to my right butt cheek.

What the . . . ?

I twisted and looked a little closer . . . "Oh my God, a leech!" I reached for it—

"*Le!*" Jaaci yelled, shooting through the water at me. She grabbed my hands and shoved them away.

I jostled in place. "Get it! Oh my God, get it!"

Jaaci held her hands up in a universal sign for hold still. She got down on her hands and knees and felt around on the river bottom.

I jostled some more, blinking soap from my stinging eyes. "Get it!"

She brought a small flat rock from the river and turned me around. Using the sharpest edge, she slowly scraped it between my butt cheek and the leech. I tried real hard to hold still, but OH MY GOD I HAD A LEECH ATTACHED TO MY BUTT!

It stung a little as I felt a tiny suction release. She took the flat rock, sliced the leech in half, and threw both halves across the river and into a bush. I watched the pieces fly through the air, hoping beyond hope that thing was dead.

I looked back at my butt cheek and saw a bloody trail. "What do I do?" Stitches? A shot? Antibacterial ointment?

Jaaci took her soap and rag and motioned for me to clean the area. I scrubbed and rubbed so hard, I nearly took my skin off.

With a laugh, Jaaci signaled for me to stop.

As quick as I could, I rinsed my hair and beelined it out of there. So much for bathing in a river. From this point on, I think I'd rather be dirty and stinky.

I dried off, dressed, and combed my hair, then followed all the girls into the jungle.

About halfway through, we passed a bunch of guys as they made their way down to the river. Carrying soap, I assumed they were going to bathe as well. I caught sight of Parrot and waved. He gave me a small smile in return. I searched the line for Jonathan or Guillermo, but didn't see them. Maybe the older guys bathed separately from the younger ones.

I realized as I stared at the line that none of the guys or girls were looking at each other. With their gazes focused down, they silently filed past not speaking, touching, or looking.

What the . . . ? How weird. I'd have to remember to ask someone about that. Someone who spoke English, that is.

We girls exited the jungle back into the clearing. It was 6:30 now, and people were up and milling around. Children laughed and played with sticks, hitting a rock around. Behind the triangular-shaped huts, women knelt in the gardens, tending to the crops. Men gathered around the big ceremonial hut, discussing matters. Underneath the square open structures, elderly women busied themselves cooking over open flames.

When did they all bathe? I found myself oddly wondering.

It occurred to me as I watched everyone how historical this event was. At no other time in history had representatives from both North and South American tribes gathered in one place. I felt truly honored to watch history in the making. In fact, it gave me goose bumps. . . . Silly, I know. But it did.

I followed the girls back inside our hut, where we deposited our things. Some of them filtered off to the gardens, others went to help the elderly women cook, and yet others disappeared inside the big ceremonial hut. I found myself standing outside, glancing around, wondering where I was supposed to go.

I still didn't see Jonathan or Guillermo. And Parrot would still be down at the river bathing. Professor Quirk was nowhere to be seen either, and I didn't know how to get to the cave and the glyphs without him. Rather than stand here idly, I made my way across the clearing over to the corral where the horses were.

Smiling at Diablo, I held out my hand. "Good morning. Did you sleep well?"

In response, he did that cute horsey growl and slowly lumbered toward me. He nuzzled my hand while I rubbed his head.

"I wish I had an apple," I cooed. "I promise to steal one from one of these gardens. That is, if they grow them in this country."

"They do." Professor Quirk stepped up beside me. "After breakfast we'll head to the cave. Sound good?"

I nodded and took a quick second to check him out now that we stood close. He'd cleaned up since I'd seen him at the river. He'd shaved and changed clothes. His freshly washed hair lay dark and smooth against his head. Through his clean glasses, I made out brilliant green eyes. He stood a little taller than me, lanky, but in okay shape. The kind of shape that came with being active, not so much from working out.

"I saw you this morning," I told him.

He furrowed his brow. "You did? Where?"

I kept my smile in check. "The river."

"When I was bathing?" he nearly squeaked.

"No." My lips curved. "When *I* was bathing. Or rather, when all of us girls were bathing."

"What?"

I laughed. "I knew you didn't see us. You were completely zoned out."

Shaking his head, he blushed. "I don't even want to think about the scene I missed out on."

I couldn't recall ever having seen a guy blush before. Well, except for Chapling.

Taking some hay from a bin, I fed a thatch to Diablo. "So, how long have you worked for the IPNC?"

"Five years. How long have you worked for the Specialists?"

"Only a year." I glanced over at him. "Quirk isn't your real name, is it?"

"No." He smiled. "Is Hannah yours?"

I stared at his smile and, oddly enough, thought he had the best teeth I'd ever seen. "No."

Quirk chuckled. "Some secret life we live, huh?"

Pulling my stare away from his gorgeous smile, I gave Diablo another thatch. "Guillermo works for the IPNC, too. But you two acted like you didn't know each other."

"We don't. IPNC's a big organization. Guillermo works solely in South America. I travel all over." Professor Quirk turned to me. "Mind if I ask you a personal question?"

Personal. I shook my head, feeling a hint of nervousness.

"How old are you?"

"Why?" I teased. "How old are you?"

One half of his mouth curved up. "I asked you first."

I smiled. "Seventeen." I didn't bother telling him I was *almost* seventeen. "And you?"

"I'm twenty-three."

"So the IPNC recruited you at eighteen?" Almost the same age as me.

"Good job, genius."

Playfully, I nudged his shoulder.

"Yep, they recruited me the day I graduated from high school," he continued. "They funded my undergraduate, masters, and doctoral studies." He returned my playful nudge. "To be recruited so young, you must have a high IQ like me. So . . . what's your IQ?"

"What?" I laughed. "What difference does that make?"

Quirk shrugged. "Mine's one sixty-one."

"Feeling competitive, are we?"

He managed to cringe a bit guiltily. "A little. So, what's yours?"

I didn't answer him right away and almost decided to lie, but told the truth instead. "One ninety-one."

Professor Quirk got really quiet, and as the seconds ticked by, he silently stared at me through unblinking green eyes.

I knew it. I shouldn't have said anything. People always thought of me as a freak of nature when they found out my true intelligence.

He swallowed. "My God, that's hot."

9

I TOOK A step back. "Wh-what?"

Professor Quirk took a step back, too. "I'm sorry. I'm so sorry. Believe I just said that I can't." He shook his head. "I mean—"

"It's okay." I laughed when it occurred to me I should probably be embarrassed or offended or something. But how could I be when this guy reminded me so much of me that it was purely laughable? Klutzy, glasses, tall, lanky, way too intelligent, and even the talking-backward-when-nervous thing. Now if he pulled out a lollipop, that'd be way too weird.

He smiled sheepishly. "You sure?"

"Believe me, I'm more than sure."

Parrot stepped up between us. "Morning," he mumbled, reaching a hand out to Abrienda, his horse, and she came over to take the berries he held.

"How'd your group bath go?" I asked Parrot.

"Fine." He shrugged, obviously still not in a talking mood.

I sighed, starting to get annoyed with his quiet demeanor. If Quirk wasn't here, I'd definitely say those exact words to Parrot. I mean, I know seeing Talon had brought back old memories, but didn't Parrot trust me? Why wouldn't he confide in me? That's what family was for. I thought we had bonded back at the ranch.

Turning, I propped my back up against the wooden corral and idly surveyed the goings-on around the village. A good solid minute went by as I watched everyone work, and my mind became curious. "I'm very interested in finding out how things work around here."

Professor Quirk hoisted himself up onto the corral, propping his boots on a low wooden barricade. "I've been here a week, and I'm just now figuring it all out. We're on Huworo land, so everything that occurs here is based on their customs."

I plucked a piece of hay from the bin and chewed on it. "Even though there are fifteen different tribal nations represented?"

Quirk nodded. "Out of respect they have to go by Huworo traditions."

Parrot turned, too, joining us in looking at the village.

"When girls and boys turn fifteen, they are moved into one of the single-men or -women huts. They stay there until they're married. Couples and families take up all the other huts. When a boy and girl get married, the whole village works together to build them their own private dwelling with a garden out back. The gardens"—Quirk motioned to them—"are maintained by wives and daughters. Meals, meetings, and festivities take place in the big circular hut in the middle."

The professor pointed to the open-square structures where older women busied themselves cooking. "The women cooking are those who have reached the age of forty and never married or women whose husbands have died. After they get done cooking, you'll see them sewing, scaling fish, doing artwork."

"What do the men do around here?" I asked. It didn't sound like they did much of anything.

"Hunt, make tools, build structures, attend meetings," Quirk answered.

"This morning when we went to bathe, none of the girls and guys looked at each other." I glanced up at him. "Why is that?"

"They're considered unclean until after morning baths," Quirk answered. "Huworo customs say unclean singles can't lay eyes on each other."

"Huh. Interesting. Where are the tribal chiefs staying?"

"Each chief was allowed to bring one representative with him." Quirk hopped down from the corral. "They're all staying in the ceremonial hut."

Jaaci stepped from the big circular structure, caught sight of me, and smiled.

I returned her smile and waved. "That's Jaaci," I told Parrot and Professor Quirk.

Sidestepping the playing children, she laughed and made her way across the dirt to where the guys and I hung out at the corral. Coming to a stop right in front of me, she rubbed her belly. *"Lirjvc?"*

"Hungry?" I nodded. "Definitely." I turned to Parrot. "This is Flint," I introduced him, using his alias. I pointed to Professor Quirk. "And Quirk."

"F-lint," she tried the name. "Ka-wirk." Smiling softly, she bowed her head to each one.

Professor Quirk stepped forward to shake her hand. "Nice to meet you."

Jaaci came out of her bow, looked at his hand, and then glanced at me, obviously at a loss. Guess they didn't shake hands in her tribe. I stepped forward and shook his hand, showing her what he wanted. Understanding, she repeated my gesture.

She switched her attention to Parrot then. "F-lint," she tried his name again, holding out her hand.

He managed a small smile as he returned her handshake.

Taking her hand back, Jaaci gestured over her shoulder. We followed her across the dirt and into the ceremonial hut.

A large circular table took up the center. On top of the table sat big steaming bowls and platters of fruit. Stacks of smaller pottery bowls and plates occupied the middle of the tabletop.

It smelled heavenly.

Situated in a U shape around the circular table sat all the tribal chiefs. I scanned their faces and zeroed in on Talon's. Sitting on a short stool, he carried on a conversation with the chief beside him and didn't even glance up at the entrance where we stood.

Behind the chiefs in the same U shape sat a row of men and behind them a row of younger boys. Children and women sat on straw cushions along the perimeter of the ceremonial hut. I caught sight of Jonathan and Guillermo in the row of men and smiled. Jonathan smiled back.

I noticed that a thick leather strap crossed Jonathan's chest, with a pouch on the end. Since we were in charge of guarding the vase, I presumed the pouch held the vase.

Jaaci showed Parrot and Professor Quirk two empty stools in the row with the younger boys, and then led me to the back to sit with the women.

A few more families filtered into the hut, taking their places depending on their age and sex.

Quietly, I sat taking in the scene. This hut had been built the same way as the one I slept in last night, only a lot bigger. Openings high up in the thatched roof let in morning light and provided ventilation. I imagined they would close those some-how if it began raining. A long table stretched the length of one wall and held hammocks and personal items that I assumed be-longed to the chiefs, since Professor Quirk said they slept in here.

For the most part, everyone spoke in a low tone with their neighbor. It put a sort of hum in the air. I estimated nearly fifty people filled the area. I caught another whiff of breakfast, and my stomach growled.

Jaaci looked over at me and laughed. And it occurred to me then that she wasn't a part of this tribe either. Her people had died, she'd found the Mother Nature vase, and here we all were. I wished she spoke English so I could ask her what her customs were. Or, for that matter, I wished I spoke her language. But that would never happen. I had not one lingual bone in my body.

I was brought abruptly from my thoughts when the oldest chief shot to his feet and began yelling something, and the whole place fell silent. He stomped over to where the food was, scooped his hand into the steaming stew, and brought out a clumpy, dripping handful. With a very angry face, he shouted something in his language.

I looked around the hut, trying to figure out what was going on.

Another chief got to his feet and, with his hands behind his back, bowed to the angry chief. He said something in a very calm voice.

The angry chief slung the stew back into the bowl and stomped across the hut and straight out the door. His assistant got up and hurried after him.

I could not *wait* to ask Parrot what was going on.

The calm chief began chanting. Two teenage boys stood, and a woman along the back did, too. Together the four of them continued chanting. It put a calm aura throughout the hut.

I glanced at Parrot and saw him bow his head in reverence.

Once they finished and took their seats, everyone began talking again. In unison, all the women stood. Following their lead, I got to my feet, too. Some of them went to the big table in the center and began ladling stew from the big steaming bowls. They placed fruit onto the small plates and served various chiefs, men, younger guys, and children. Then they went back and got more stew and fruit, brought it back to where we women stood, and began eating.

For a minute there, I thought maybe they were going to serve me.

More women left our line and repeated what the others had done. I could only assume maybe they were serving their families.

Jaaci left our line on round three, motioning for me to follow. Copying what I'd seen the other women do, I ladled stew into bowls and piled fruit on plates. With a bowl in each hand I turned to the crowd and realized I'd caught the attention of quite a few people.

Not like everyone fell quiet to stare or anything, but definitely a dozen or more men and women were looking at me. Suddenly self-conscious, I glanced at Jonathan, and he motioned me over.

He took the food from me. "They're staring at your blond hair," he whispered. "Don't worry about it, you're doing fine."

Guillermo took his food, too. "Some of the older men believe blond hair means you've been touched by the gods."

I rolled my eyes. "Did you tell them in America most people think blond hair means you're stupid?"

Guillermo laughed at that.

"What happened with that older chief?" I whispered.

"Now's not the time," Jonathan answered. "I'll tell you later."

With a nod, I headed back to the food and caught sight of Jaaci serving Parrot and the professor. I ladled stew into a bowl, piled fruit on a plate, and balancing both, I turned to take my seat and ran smack into Jaaci.

My stew went down the front of her dress and my fruit went flying through the air.

"Oh, my God!" I reached for Jaaci. "I'm so sorry."

Someone shouted something, and I whipped my head to the left to see Talon standing. With a clenched jaw, he grabbed a couple pieces of my fruit off him and, staring at me, slung them to the floor.

I sucked in a breath.

Shouting something else, he took a step toward me, and simultaneously every one of my team members got to their feet.

Talon dragged his dark, menacing gaze off me and looked at each of my team members. Jonathan, Guillermo, Quirk, and finally Parrot.

A couple of quiet seconds ticked by.

Switching his gaze back to me, Talon slowly sat down, and in my peripheral vision I saw my team members take their seats, too.

Gradually, the entire hut began eating again.

Swallowing, my heart pounding, I glanced at Jonathan. He nodded for me to get some food.

Jaaci touched my arm and I turned to her. "I'm so sorry," I said.

Smiling as if she understood me, she shook her head and waved me off. But I couldn't help but stare at her beautiful dress that was messed up because of me.

She indicated the food, and we served ourselves. It could have been my imagination, but I swore I felt Talon's glare boring a hole into my back.

I didn't chance a look in his direction as I followed Jaaci back to our straw mats. We sat down and dug into the food.

I scooped a hunk of meat out of the stew and chomped down, loving the mild spicy, oniony taste. "What is this?" I motioned to my bowl.

Jaaci shook her head, clearly not understanding my question.

I tried again, scooping up some of the meat. "What?"

She nodded, *"Kafferw,"* and pointed to the other side of the hut where an elderly woman sat with a rather ugly-looking monkey on her shoulder.

I paused, then I froze as I realized, *"Monkey?* This is monkey stew?"

Jaaci smiled.

Suddenly, my stomach didn't feel so well. Swallowing back rising bile, I slowly put the bowl down and pushed it out of my way. I covered my face with my hands and told myself to not get sick.

My whole body warmed, and each voice in the room seem to amplify as I willed my stomach to settle.

People talked.

Metal spoons scraped against pottery bowls.

Someone laughed.

With my hands still covering my face, I concentrated on breathing in and out through my mouth so I wouldn't smell the oniony stew.

Jaaci put her hand on my back. *"Cei enoc?"*

Still breathing through my mouth, I shook my head. I had no idea what she'd asked me. Without looking at her, I spoke. "I need some fresh air."

I got up and didn't look at a single soul as I left the ceremonial hut. It was probably rude to leave in the middle of a meal, but frankly, I didn't care. It was either that, or the whole tribe would have seen my breakfast coming back up. And after spilling food on Jaaci, I didn't need any more humiliation.

Standing outside, I closed my eyes and drew in a long breath of air. "You will not get sick," I told myself on exhale. I inhaled again. "You will not get sick," on exhale. I repeated that over and over, and, when I felt steady enough, I opened my eyes.

"Better?"

I jerked around. "Professor Quirk? How long have you been there?"

"Long enough. I take it you found out we were eating mo—"

"Don't." I held my hand up. "Don't say it."

He smiled and paused. "I'm glad someone else is as klutzy as me," he said, changing the subject.

I rolled my eyes. "You have no idea."

He laughed at that.

Out of the corner of my eye, I saw the old chief who had stomped out of breakfast. I nodded toward him politely. He returned my nod, and when he was out of sight, I turned to Quirk. "Any idea what that yelling and stew flinging was all about?"

Quirk nodded. "Yeah. Their tribe considers the monkey a sacred animal."

"Yikes. No wonder he was so mad."

"It was a pretty big insult to serve monkey. This faux pas can affect the relationship between these two tribes for years. But that's not our problem. We have glyphs to decode. You ready to see the cave and the drawings?"

Eagerly, I nodded. "Definitely."

I jogged over to the hut I'd slept in and retrieved my laptop.

Quirk met me outside. "Here," he said, handing me a cloth pouch hanging from the end of a thin rope. "It's for the bugs." He held up the one he wore around his neck. "One of the Huworo people gave it to me the first day I got here. I don't know what's in it—some herbs, I think—but whatever it is, it works great."

"Thanks." I put it around my neck. "Too bad I didn't have this last night. Termite guts are about as disgusting as I want to get."

He laughed at that and motioned me into the jungle.

"So you've been here a week," I struck up a conversation.

He stepped over a downed tree. "Yes. I've been holed up in the cave sketching the glyphs. It will make your job a lot easier since I already have half the cave sketched. You can scan my drawings into your computer and plug them into your translation program. Which"—he glanced over at me—"I've been extremely eager to see. There's no other program like it, I hear."

I nodded a little, feeling a swell of pride at my creation. Too bad it had to remain top secret.

"Too bad it has to remain top secret." Professor Quirk ducked under a low branch. "That would be an amazing thing to introduce into the world of historians."

I blinked. "I was just thinking that." How weird.

He smiled a little. "What made you create the program? Are you interested in cave drawings?"

"A couple of our agents are on a mission where cave drawings are involved. I thought the program would make things go smoother for them." Unsure of how much I could say, I stopped there.

Quirk nodded, but didn't ask any more questions.

We continued on, and out of the corner of my eye, I noticed he was staring at me. Suddenly, he ran straight into a bush and caught himself as he stumbled over it.

I smiled and reached for him. "You okay?"

Quirk sighed. "Yes."

I smiled again at his exasperated tone. He *did* say he was as klutzy as me.

Trying to regain his composure, he cleared his throat. "It's amazing that the whereabouts of this cave has never been documented. If Jaaci's dying father hadn't told her about it and the Mother Nature vase, it'd still be a historical mystery. I studied all about it in my course work. Most of my professors felt it was a legend." Quirk looked back at me. "Have you seen the vase yet?"

I shook my head.

"The Huworo chief gave it to your leader to guard, the guy with the eye patch. What's his name again?"

"Shane," I answered, using Jonathan's alias.

The professor nodded. "I've analyzed the inscriptions and have estimated that the glyphs date back to AD 1100."

"Wow."

"You can say that again."

"Wow."

Professor Quirk laughed.

I followed him around a huge tree trunk. "The drawings are supposed to reveal a key piece of information about the vase. Any ideas yet?"

He shook his head. "This is my specialty. But to be honest, I've never seen anything like it—the pattern, that is. I've seen the symbols before, but they don't seem to follow a pattern, or at least one that I know of."

"Hopefully, that's where my program will come in."

"Hopefully," he agreed.

We emerged from the jungle and came to an abrupt stop. In front of us stretched a very *long* swinging rope bridge, connecting the ledge we stood on to a ledge *way* across a *huge* gap in land.

Swallowing, I took in the void between the two ledges and estimated it to be about a mile. "Wh-where's the cave?"

Professor Quirk pointed across the gap. "Over there."

I closed my eyes. *Figures.* Nothing's ever easy in this business. "H-how far down?"

"C—"

"Wait." I held up my hand. "I don't want to know."

He stepped onto the swinging bridge. "Come on."

Holding on to the ropes that encased the bridge, Quirk began making his way across. As he did, I studied the engineering of the clearly unstable structure. Wood planks served as stepping pieces, positioned about an inch apart. Rope wound the ends of the wood and knotted into the thick twine of the netted walls and handrails. The bridge appeared wide enough for only one person at a time.

I'd feel a lot better if something on the swinging structure resembled steel. Or concrete. Or something else equally stable. No wonder we'd had balancing lessons in PT.

Roughly halfway across, Quirk glanced back at me. "Come on," he yelled.

"I'm going to wait until you get across." One person's weight was enough for this spindly thing.

I heard him mumble, "Chicken," and narrowed my eyes. I'd show him chicken.

Feeling a surge of courage, I grabbed on to the handholds and stepped onto the first wood plank. My confidence quickly dwindled as the bridge swung slightly. I swallowed again, closed my eyes, and told myself not to look down.

That was like trying to tell me not to peek at Chapling's new subelesup code.

I knew I *would* look down, so I opened my eyes to go ahead and get it over with, and my heart stopped.

This canyon, or whatever it was called, disappeared into nothingness, just like before when I'd been on Diablo crossing the ledge. Tightening my grip on the ropes, I felt my body make the bridge shake again and tried to loosen my muscles, but couldn't.

I stared as daylight filtered down into the canyon, becoming darker and darker with the depth, until only blackness colored the area.

"Stop holding your breath," the professor yelled.

I realized then I wasn't breathing and gulped in some air. With stiff, unbending muscles, I commanded my legs to move and dragged first my right boot and then my left back off the wood and onto the ground. I glanced up to see that Quirk had made it all the way across. I thought he was supposed to be klutzy.

"Are you kidding me?" the professor yelled.

I lifted my right fist, and for the first time in my life, I flipped somebody off.

He barked a laugh in response.

It made me want to flip him off again, double time.

Taking a breath, I stared hard at the bridge and a ghost of a memory floated through my mind. I saw four-year-old me holding my mom's hand. We stood on a rope-and-wood bridge that stretched about twenty feet between two pieces of land. A river bubbled ten feet below us.

My mother and I wore coats, gloves, and scarves, and my dad stood on the bridge, too, facing us. Laughing, he shifted his body weight and made the bridge swing. My mom laughed, too, and tried to tell him to stop but couldn't get the words out between her giggles. I squealed and squeezed my mom's hand and squealed some more.

"You coming or what?" Professor Quirk yelled, snapping me from the memory.

I felt a smile curving my lips and breathed a content sigh. Holding on to that memory, I stepped back onto the swinging bridge and walked all the way across. I didn't look down once and instead recalled the rest of that afternoon with my parents. My family had hiked through the woods, picnicked on a big flat rock, drove the winding mountainous road to the top, and stood looking out over a valley with colorful autumn trees.

"Wasn't so bad, was it?" Quirk asked, as I stepped off the other side of the bridge. "I saw you smiling."

I narrowed my eyes. "Optical illusion."

"Truth is, first time I did it I was scared out of mind."

"Thanks for telling me that *after* I made it across."

Quirk shot me a not-so-innocent smile. "We're almost there." He led me back into the jungle and around the biggest rock I'd ever seen.

Stopping around the back side of this boulder, he pointed to a dark opening in a hill covered by a thick green vine. "The cave." Leaning down, Quirk stepped into the darkness of the opening. "Let's do this."

10

ᗡuᴄᴋiᴎg ᗡoᴡᴎ. I followed the professor into the dark cave.

Quirk flipped on a flashlight. He swept the beam along the walls and ceiling, illuminating a tunnel that stretched in front of us. "This goes for fifty feet and then it opens up into the room we'll be working from."

"*Fifty feet?* Now's probably not a good time to tell you I'm a little bit claustrophobic."

"No. Not really. However," he sighed, "I am as well. More than a little."

"Well, you've been here a week," I tried to reason. "Surely you've gotten used to it."

"Yeah. Not so much."

It occurred to me then. "What the heck did you specialize in glyphs for if you're claustrophobic? Hello? Cave drawings are generally found in caves."

Quirk turned to me. "You can stop talking any time now."

I motioned him forward. "Lead the way."

In our crouched stance, we hobbled down the tunnel. I flicked my gaze from wall, to ceiling, to floor, keeping an eye out for bugs, bats, or anything else suspicious. "I thought caves were supposed to be dirty. I don't see any bugs or slimy things."

"This is a dry cave. There's been no water intrusion. If my research holds true, this is the first time that this cave has seen climate since it was sealed shut a century ago. Plus, I swept it out."

"You swept it out?"

"I don't like an unclean working environment."

"A little OCD, are we?"

Quirk shrugged. "A little." He got down on his hands and knees.

"What are you doing?"

He swept the flashlight down the length of the ceiling showing where it dropped dramatically toward the floor. "We crawl the rest of the way."

Great. I slid my laptop around my body to rest on my back and became one with the floor. We crawled down the clean, freshly swept tunnel on our bellies. I found myself appreciating Professor Quirk's obsessive cleaning habits.

"It's amazing that Jaaci fearlessly entered this cave to live out her father's dying wish to retrieve the Mother Nature vase. Can you imagine?"

Quirk didn't respond to my comment. "Professor Quirk?"

His shaky breathing echoed back to me. I lifted my head and stared at his boots as he belly-crawled in front of me. "Professor Quirk?"

"K-keep talking."

Oh boy, the last thing I needed was a wigged-out professor. I racked my brain for something to talk about and came up empty. Of all the times for me to come up empty. And then it occurred to me, "Uh-huh, look who's scared now, Mr. I-Made-It-Across-the-Bridge."

He stopped moving. "Are you making fun of me?"

I smiled. "Yes, I am."

Quirk started moving again. "I've decided I don't like you anymore."

His teasing tone made me smile even bigger. "So I was thinking, it's kind of weird to call you 'Professor,' don't ya think? Professor sounds like a title someone older should have. Someone bald and pudgy. How about I just call you Quirk? Although, whoever came up with Quirk for your cover could have done a better job. I mean, really, Quirk? Come on."

"Quirk's fine."

"Good. Quirk, it is."

A few seconds went by, and I heard his breathing pick up and thought he might be getting a little nervous again. "Um, tell me where you're from."

"S-Seattle."

"Seattle, huh? I hear there's lots of rain there."

He didn't answer.

"So, um, you said the IPNC recruited you and paid for your college. How'd they find you?"

"High school test scores."

"Ah, yes, the ole test scores. Do you think you'll stay with the IPNC or transfer to another branch?"

"Don't know."

I searched my brain for another question and all I came up with was, "What's your favorite color?"

On and on I talked, asking him ridiculous questions, while we *slowly* crawled our way down the tunnel. It seemed like it took forever. And I had to admit, I did quite the bang-up job of mindlessly chattering and keeping Quirk's brain preoccupied. Well, to me it wasn't mindless chatter. I very thoroughly explained the filament of a nonsuffixion NFD syntagma.

Sometime later Quirk slid from the tunnel. "We're here," he breathed.

I crawled out after him, feeling just as relieved as he sounded.

"Listen," he said as he turned around and touched my arm. "Thanks for your help back there."

I shrugged. "No biggie."

"And I now know more about NFD syn-whatever than I ever thought possible."

I smiled. "Glad to help."

He returned my smile, but didn't make another comment. Quiet seconds ticked by as we stared into each other's shadowed faces. Slowly, his smile faded, and his eyes dropped to my lips. In that moment I knew things had shifted between us, and my stomach started uncontrollably whirling.

I looked away.

"Do you, um, have a boyfriend?"

Still not looking at him, I slowly nodded as my heart raced around in my chest. I didn't think my voice would come out even if I tried.

"Lucky guy."

I smiled, an image of David coming to my mind.

Clearing his throat, Quirk shifted onto his feet and away from me, and I glanced up. I couldn't help but compare him to David.

Quirk was the kind of guy who would understand my brain, kind of like Chapling did. My mentor and I connected on a whole other level. It would be that way with Quirk. I adored David, but that was the one thing missing. Sometimes I felt like he really just didn't "get" me. He thought I was more cute, adorable. He thought smart chicks were cool.

I closed my eyes to clear my head. Why was I even comparing Quirk to David? David was great.

"This room is fifteen feet in diameter," Quirk said, interrupting my thoughts.

Using the flashlight, he walked away from me. I watched as he paced the perimeter of the circular room, leaning down to turn on battery-operated lanterns. Section by section the room began to glow, and simultaneously my jaw dropped.

Cave drawings covered every inch of the walls, ceiling, and floor. Row after row of engraved symbols. Column after column of etched images. Every intricate carving looked to be about the same size. There wasn't an untouched part of the room. It was breathtaking. "No wonder you love this so much," I said in awe.

With the room glowing now, Quirk stood in the center, making a slow circle as he took everything in. "I've been here a week, and I still get the shivers every time I look at it."

I rubbed my hands up and down my arms, sort of feeling those shivers, too. Like we were on sacred ground or something.

Laughing, Quirk looked at me. "It's amazing to think someone stood here in AD 1100 and did this." He pointed to the ceiling. "Look at the intricacy of the animals there." He pointed to the floor. "And this row . . . I can't get over it." He turned another circle. "This room is ancient code, and you and I are going to break it. We're going to make history!"

I smiled at his excitement, even though I really didn't feel it. Whoever created and hid this room obviously never wanted it to be found. I felt like I might be messing with the gods or something.

"Know where the vase was?" Quirk asked.

"No."

He crossed the room to where a small rock ledge protruded from the wall. "It was sitting right here, as peaceful as you please."

"Hmmm . . ." Quirk continued studying the circular room, and I realized he was zoning out.

Ready to try my new program, I unzipped my laptop case. "Well, let's get busy."

"Did you know that many carvings are considered sacred?" Quirk asked, clearly not having heard what I'd said.

"Yes, actually, I do." I pulled my laptop out. "I'm ready when you are."

"The writings began about five thousand years ago. The first ones were written in three languages: Greek, demotic, and hieroglyphic. A French Egyptologist recognized the word *Ptolemy*, which was encased in a cartouche, and was able to match it up to the Greek spelling." Quirk put a finger in the air. "Ptolemy, by the way, was a ruler of Egypt."

"Mmm-hmmm." I plugged a battery into the power jack, and turned on my laptop. "Now just show me where your drawings are and—"

"Some hieroglyphs stand for words, others sounds, and yet others syllables. Depending on which way the graphics point determines how you read them. Left to right or right to left. They can also be read up and down." He tapped his fingers together. "Just remember when you're deciphering, the hieroglyphs match up to sounds, not letters."

I resisted the urge to tell him that I already knew all this. I had to know it in order to create my translation program. "Um, can we just—"

"Egyptians focused on consonant sounds, not vowels." He tapped his forehead. "Although there were determinatives that you could tack onto the end to give a hint to its meaning."

"Quirk?"

"Oh." He put that finger in the air again. "There're all different kinds of symbols. You can use birds, arms, legs, leaves, worms, squiggly lines, bowls, lions, squares . . . but I've been rattling on about Egypt. Now, Mayan drawings are even more exciting . . ."

My eyes glassed over. I imagined this was what other people felt like when I got off on one of my computer tangents. "Quirk?"

". . . the pictorial intricacy and calligraphic style of Mayan glyphs are, in my opinion, like no other . . ."

With a sigh, I dug out two lollipops from my laptop case. I unwrapped both, put one in my mouth, crossed the room to Quirk, and stuck the other in his mouth. He fell quiet. Like a baby, he sucked the lollipop, still studying the room.

"Now if you would please give me your drawings, I can get them scanned and start deciphering this code."

Pulling the lollipop from his mouth, he looked at me. "This is really good. What is this, raspberry?"

I nodded. "The sketches?"

"Oh, yes. I left my portfolio in here yesterday." It sat propped against the wall. He opened it and handed me a stack of wax paper. "Be careful. Those are originals."

Propping myself up against the wall, I laid the stack beside me and took my ultra-thin, extremely cool, portable wand scanner from my laptop case. Page by page I input the images into my program while Quirk stood with his back to me, sketching parts of the room he hadn't gotten to yet.

We worked for hours, stopping only once to change batteries in the lanterns and eat meat jerky he'd brought. I didn't ask what kind of meat. I didn't want to know.

By my estimation, he'd managed to sketch half the room in the week he'd been here. Which meant it would take him another whole week to sketch the rest, right in time with the length of the mission. Hopefully, my program wouldn't need all the glyphs to decode the message.

A few hours later, he put his portfolio back together. "I need fresh air and real food. And it's going to be dark soon. I don't want to go back through the jungle at nighttime." Quirk came over and sat down beside me. "What's your program got so far?"

After a few clicks, I studied the screen . . . and my whole body sank. "Nothing."

"It's okay." Quirk shrugged. "Maybe tomorrow."

"Maybe."

We extinguished the lanterns, crawled back through the tunnel entrance, and traversed the swinging bridge. As we made our way through the jungle, we ran into Jonathan.

"I tried to get over to the cave," Jonathan began, "but Guillermo and I had to go into town for an emergency conference call with the IPNC and our top guy at the Specialists."

By "top guy" I knew he meant TL, but because of Quirk, Jonathan didn't say his name.

"Intel told us weeks ago that two chiefs were planning to steal the vase. Last night another message was intercepted.

Unfortunately, we still don't have the identity of the chiefs, but the message indicated a hit man has been hired. For whom, we're unsure."

"Hit man?" I asked. "You mean someone from one of the tribes?"

"Yes. For all we know, he or she could be part of the talks, a Huworo native . . . no telling. But all the chiefs know you're in the cave decoding the glyphs for a key piece of information about the vase, presumably its rightful owner. We do not believe one of our team members is in immediate danger, but watch each other's backs."

Quirk and I nodded our understanding.

"And do your best to decipher the code as soon as possible."

I didn't think now was a good time to tell Jonathan my program had given me nothing today.

"How's your program doing?" he asked.

"So far so good," I sort of lied.

"Do you have anything yet?"

"Hopefully, by tomorrow." I dodged a direct answer to his question, not wanting to admit I had doubts, *serious* doubts, that my software would come through. I glanced down at the pouch he wore. "Can we see the vase?"

Carefully he removed the leather pouch from his body and handed it to me. I undid the tied strap and pulled out the vase wrapped heavily in thick layers of protective cloth. One by one I unfolded the layers, and as I got closer and closer to revealing the artifact, it occurred to me I probably shouldn't be doing this. I might break it. And then where would that leave everything?

GiGi ruins history.

I handed the wad back to Jonathan. "You do it. I don't trust myself."

With big, confident fingers, he unfolded the wrapping and held it out for us to see. Quirk and I both moved closer, neither one of us touching it. Usually things appeared different in person, but to my surprise, the vase looked just like it had up on the screen back at the ranch.

I glanced up at Jonathan. "Aren't you worried you might break it or lose it or someone might steal it?"

He arched an incredulous brow, as if that was the silliest thing to worry about.

Okay, it probably was for someone like Jonathan or TL. But me? It was definitely something to worry about. I couldn't imagine being given this priceless artifact to guard.

Jonathan wrapped it back up. "Let's call it a day. I want to touch base with Flint," he said, using Parrot's alias.

We followed Jonathan back to the Huworo village.

Quirk walked toward the single-men hut, and, when he was out of hearing range, Jonathan turned to me. "When I was in town, I told TL about what happened back in the airport security shack yesterday. He wants you to get that drawing of that woman to Chapling as soon as possible."

"Sure. No problem."

"And"—Jonathan cleared his throat—"I have a message for you from David."

My stomach swirled. "David?"

"He was on the conference call earlier. He said he tried texting you, but it didn't go through."

Huh. I checked my cell and saw I had no signal. Even with our new satellite chips, the jungle still made it difficult. I looked up at Jonathan in expectation of David's message.

He managed to look a bit embarrassed. "David says hi."

I waited for the rest of the message, but Jonathan said nothing. "Hi?" I asked. "That's it?"

Jonathan gave a terse nod. "I told him I was not a telegram service and to limit his message to one word."

I narrowed my eyes. "How generous of you."

With another nod, Jonathan headed off in the opposite direction. "I'll be back in a few minutes to head over to the talks. Remember the drawing. Try to find a signal for your computer so you can send the scan to Chapling."

"Yeah. No problem," I said, preoccupied.

Hi. One word. David was on the other side of the world and yet he still, in one word, managed to make me feel like he was right here.

With a sigh, I took my laptop and cell phone in the hopes of finding a nearby signal. Someplace high up. I looked up into the thick foliage and turned a slow circle. Maybe I could climb a tree?

"What are you doing?" Quirk asked.

I jumped. "I thought you went back to your hut."

He smiled. "I did. But I wanted to go for a walk. Need to clear my head of all those cave drawings. So what are you doing? Looking for monkeys?"

"Ha-ha." I held up my laptop. "I need a signal."

Quirk nodded. "I know the perfect place." He started walking, and I followed. We went across the village and past the corral and then came to a stop. He pointed up. "Watchtower."

I craned my neck all the way back and sure enough at the top of a very *tall* tree sat a watchtower. I squinted my eyes and made out a man, presumably the watch person. I swallowed. "That's really far up."

Quirk shrugged. "You said you wanted a signal."

"What are you two doing?" Jonathan asked, coming up behind us.

Quirk pointed up. "She said she needed a signal."

Jonathan looked up and whistled. "That should do it." He motioned toward the ceremonial hut. "However, I think you should come with me to the talks instead. It'll be interesting for you to witness your teammate in action."

I held up my laptop. "Do the other thing later then?"

Jonathan nodded.

"I didn't realize I was allowed in the talks. I thought only natives could attend."

"Only the chiefs and the translators are allowed to speak. Anyone else can witness it." Jonathan started walking slowly toward the big circular structure, and Quirk and I stepped in line beside him.

"How are the talks going?" I asked.

"Every chief has valid documentation to prove the Mother Nature vase belonged to his tribe at one time in history. None of the chiefs is willing to give up his rights to the artifact." Jonathan shook his head. "It's wearing Flint out."

I sighed. "I hate hearing that."

Jonathan stopped at the entrance to the ceremonial hut. "They are very interested in finding out what those glyphs say exactly."

"We're trying our best," Quirk commented, motioning to the opening in the hut. "Shall we?"

Jonathan and I followed Quirk inside. Like breakfast this morning, everyone sat in designated areas, depending on their gender and age. Parrot, however, sat right dead center with the chiefs. The personal translators sat behind them.

Jonathan took his spot beside Guillermo, and I found an empty straw mat beside Jaaci along the back wall. She smiled at me as I situated myself beside her. I located Talon among the chiefs. He sat directly across the U shape from Parrot, right in Parrot's line of sight. And although Talon's back was to me, it appeared as if he was staring straight at Parrot.

I switched my gaze to Parrot and found him looking everywhere *but* in Talon's direction.

A chief wearing a nose ring lifted an old parchment rolled and secured with a black leather strap. *"Lu ymbarsiqr misysac va gyc sga tyra em ioq nirrarreim em dedsaam svamsu sgqaa . . ."*

He continued in his native tongue, and my brain went numb

trying to keep up. A minute later the chief finished, and everyone turned their attention to Parrot.

Parrot took a second or two, probably trying to translate what was said in his own brain, and then spoke, "My ancestors noted that we had the vase in our possession in fifteen twenty-three. Mother Nature relieved the great drought of that year. We had the best crops ever. And then the Bidum warriors raided our village and stole the vase."

The chiefs' personal translators leaned forward and whispered into their ears, converting Parrot's English into their chief's language.

"Xjisit auys qsuug na qiuqmf seofif auys wommehf?" shouted a chief with black dots tattooed over his face, chest, and arms.

Everyone turned to Parrot. He took a second . . . "Where's your proof that my people raided your village?"

The translators simultaneously whispered into their chiefs' ears.

"Sgys tyra qefgsdokka zakimfr . . ." The chief with the nose ring spoke again.

Everyone turned to Parrot. He took a second . . . "That vase rightfully belongs to my people. Stealing it doesn't legally make it yours."

The translators simultaneously whispered into their chiefs' ears.

"Oyq," a chief wearing a colorful robe grunted. *"Xir xycepy oeip . . ."*

Everyone turned to Parrot. "Yes, but before your people had it, we had it. Where's your proof that your people didn't steal it from us?"

On and on the talks went, with no hope of resolution in sight.

And after a while, I found myself studying Parrot. To any person who really didn't know him, they would think he was fine by looking at him. Calm, controlled, patient. But I'd known Parrot nearly a year, and although he hid it well, I detected the exhaustion and stress in him. Little things like reaching up to rub his temple, blinking slow from dry eyes, the fatigue in his voice, and the way he kept forcing himself to sit up straight.

I couldn't imagine so many voices circling around in my head, bumping into each other, pushing and shoving for space. I'd probably go insane with the overload.

I wished I had the power to call an end to things and give him a break.

Suddenly, a deep grunt vibrated through the hut, and I snapped to attention.

A chief with very long hair shot angrily to his feet. He yelled across the U shape at the chief with the black-dot tattoos, and that chief got to his feet, too.

Back and forth they yelled, and it sounded as if they were using some of the same words. Parrot got to his feet and tried to keep up, but with their fast exchange and loud voices, Parrot's voice was overpowered.

Then the two chiefs charged at each other, and I sucked in a breath.

Other chiefs and assistants rushed the two who were about to fight and pulled them apart. They were all shouting over one another. The chief with the long hair shoved others out of his way and stormed from the hut. The chief with the tattoo plopped back down on his stool. And then slowly everyone trickled back to their seats.

I looked at each of my team members, and they seemed as caught off guard as me.

Things quieted and, just as I thought the talks would begin again, Talon stood. Up to this point he'd been quiet. For the first time since I'd come in, Parrot gazed straight across the U and into Talon's eyes.

And then Talon lifted a finger and pointed it right at Parrot.

TO PARROT'S CREDIT, he kept his gaze passively fastened on Talon as if he were any other chief standing there pointing his finger. Parrot showed no signs of recognition, no signs of fear, only a hint of question floated in his eyes.

All the chiefs stared at Talon waiting for him to speak.

"Baet pawkot yaeng doe yote ratag," he finally said, before turning and walking straight out of the ceremonial hut.

The chiefs silently looked at one another, clearly wondering what was going on. I switched my attention to Parrot and found him looking straight at me.

The same chief who had chanted at this morning's breakfast stood and said something in his language.

Everyone looked at Parrot. "Today's events are over," he translated.

The chiefs' assistants whispered the translation into their ears, and then everyone started getting up and filing out of the hut. With my laptop in tow, I made a beeline for Parrot.

"Let's talk," I said, grabbing his arm, not giving him a chance to say no.

We wove our way through the departing crowd, across the village, and stopped at the corral. Our horses Diablo and Abrienda came right over.

"Tell me what's going on," I demanded, not giving him the time to decide if he wanted to talk to me or not. I'd been more than patient with Parrot's silence, but it was evident I'd have to pull information from him.

And I thought *I* was hard to talk to.

I planted my hand on my hip. "I want to know the story of you and Talon." I wasn't being nosy, or a bully. I knew if Parrot didn't talk to someone, he was going to explode from the stress. "What did he just say to you?"

He turned and stalked off.

What the . . . ?

I stalked after him. "Stop."

Blatantly ignoring me, Parrot marched right into the jungle.

"Parrot! Stop!"

He threw his hand up, telling me to bug off.

It only fueled my fire. I ran to catch up, dug my fingers in his arm, and spun him around. I jabbed my finger in his face. "Now listen. I'm sick of you keeping everything secret. This is starting to affect the mission. If I have to be concerned about Talon, that maybe he is the hit man, then I need to know. I want you to talk. *Now.*"

Parrot jabbed his finger right back in my face. "And I'm sick of you bugging me. This has nothing to do with the mission. Just leave me alone!"

"No."

His face hardened. "Get. Out. Of. My. Face," he gritted.

"No," I ground out through clenched teeth, fully aware I was pushing *both* of us beyond the limit.

Parrot growled, a very out-of-character reaction. He turned away from me and, with fisted hands, let out a loud yell. It echoed through the jungle, and my stomach clenched with the primal sound of it. Like all the frustration and anger over his entire life had just erupted from his body.

With another yell, he spun and kicked a tree. And kicked it again.

I reached for him. "Parrot, stop. You're going to break your toes."

He turned away from me and put his hands over his face. "Please. Just leave me alone."

Putting my laptop down, I stepped up behind him and wrapped my arms tight around him. He tried to pull away, and I squeezed him harder.

Parrot inhaled a choppy breath. "Oh, God." Another choppy breath and then a quiet sob. The painful sound broke my heart.

Laying my cheek on his shoulder, I held on tight, while his body shook with sadness. I wondered if this was the first time he'd ever had a good cry.

Minutes passed, and I continued holding him.

He took some deep breaths, trying to get control of his emotions.

Finally, he sniffed. "Do you remember the day we all first met?" he mumbled into his hands.

I nodded against his shoulder, not wanting to let him go yet.

Parrot pulled away, and I reluctantly released him. With his back to me, he used his T-shirt to wipe his face. A few seconds passed as he gained more control. "I said I was taken in by the police for flying in a restricted airspace." He turned around and looked me right in the eyes. "I lied."

My heart paused a beat. "What do you mean you lied?"

He studied my face, as if trying to figure out exactly how much he could or would say to me.

I reached out and gripped his hand and looked him deep in the eyes. "Listen to me. Nothing you tell me will change who you are. Be truthful. Don't worry. None of us have had a past worth bragging about."

Parrot dropped his gaze to our clasped hands and quietly contemplated them. "I used to work for Talon," he said a few seconds later. "I interpreted deals for him. Slave trade. Mostly young girls." His voice broke.

I put my hand over my mouth.

He brought his pain-filled eyes up to meet mine. "It's not something I'm proud of. I was so ashamed. I never wanted any of you guys to know."

I rubbed my thumb over his knuckles. "It's okay."

Parrot sniffed and used his free hand to wipe his eyes. "Talon told me he knew where my mother was. And if I worked for him for six months, he'd reunite me with her."

"Oh, Parrot." I would do anything, too, to bring back my parents, if only for a few special moments with them.

"I didn't know it was slave trade. I never knew what the 'cargo' was."

I saw regret in his face, along with a hint of disgust at what he'd been involved in.

He looked up into my eyes. "I need you to believe that."

"I do." Closing the small space between us, I gave him a hug. "You know I do." I stepped away. "Do you have any news about your mom?" I asked, hopeful.

Parrot shook his head, his eyes welling up again. "No."

"Why isn't Talon in jail?"

"Because I refused to testify. Talon's the only one who knows where my mom is. When she's found, I'll testify and put him away."

"Why not just go ahead and testify?"

Adamantly, he shook his head. "No. I won't do anything until she's found. I'm not going to take any chances. TL knows that." Parrot grasped my upper arm. "Promise me you'll be careful and stay away from Talon." He gave my arm a little shake. "Promise."

The conviction in his voice gave me a chill. "I promise."

Nodding, he stepped away.

"What did he say to you back there at the hut?"

"That my mom would be so proud."

"Oh, no."

Parrot sighed. "I know. He knows who I am. Why else would he say that?"

I nodded my agreement. "We have to tell Jonathan."

Together we turned, and at the exact same second caught sight of Talon standing behind a tree watching us. Parrot and I froze as we stared back.

Talon made no expression, made no attempt to hide. He headed off diagonal to us, disappearing farther into the jungle.

We watched him go until we couldn't see him anymore.

"Do you think he heard us?"

Parrot closed his eyes and rubbed his forehead. "He may have."

"Where do you think he's going?" I asked.

"I have no idea."

Cautiously, we made our way back toward the village as darkness settled in around us. It was no wonder Parrot didn't want to come on this mission. His specialty, his gift, had been abused and used against him. And now here he had to face the same man who'd maltreated his talents. The man who knew where his mother was.

"Thanks for being honest and talking with me," I said.

Parrot smiled a little in response.

As we exited the jungle, Jonathan came right toward us. "Where have you been? I don't want you two going off alone. With the new intel, I'm not taking any chances."

"Yes, sir," we answered.

"Parrot needed some time to think, and I followed him," I explained. "But as we were heading back, we saw Talon. He must have followed us into the jungle."

"What happened?" Jonathan asked.

"Nothing," Parrot answered. "He watched us silently and then headed off in the opposite direction. We left immediately and were coming to tell you when you met us."

"Where'd he go?" Jonathan asked.

We shrugged.

Jonathan nodded. "Okay, I'll get Guillermo on that. He knows this jungle better than anyone. What did Talon say to you back at the hut?"

Parrot pressed his fingers to his temples. "That my mother would be so proud."

Jonathan furrowed his brow. "Not good. It's a little too coincidental. You both need to be on alert. Be very careful. If Talon *does* know it's Parrot, there's no telling what he may do." Jonathan turned to me. "You must keep an eye on your laptop at all times. And it's set with the highest security settings, correct?"

"Yes, sir."

With a nod, Jonathan glanced up at the watchtower. "You still have to send Chapling the scan, but I don't want you going up there. That's too far up without safety gear. We'll find a signal somewhere else."

Behind Jonathan, something moved, and I peeked around him to see the Huworo chief striding toward us across the clearing. Two men walked with him, staying one step behind. With stern faces, bald heads, and yellow painted chests, they carried spears in front of them.

"Um, Jonathan," I said, and he turned around.

The Huworo chief came to a stop right in front of us. He nodded first to me, then Parrot, and then to Jonathan. *"Ruf Lepre olb Qerif Okupazol Ojjazolu . . ."* he spoke in his language.

"The North and South American Alliance," Parrot translated, "has decided the vase will be more secure under the watchful eyes of my trained guards."

Jonathan didn't respond for a second. "I assure you, I am highly skilled in the job you have hired me for."

Parrot translated.

The Huworo chief repeated himself, motioning for the guards to take the pouch and the vase from Jonathan.

Jonathan held up his hands to let the guards know he would cooperate and then slipped the pouch over his head and gave it to the Huworo chief.

The chief nodded, turned, and headed back across the clearing.

I looked at Jonathan and knew without him saying one single word that he was really PO'ed. "What's going on?"

Jonathan shook his head. "Don't know. But I don't like it at all."

"Couldn't you do anything?" Parrot asked as we walked back to the village.

"No. The alliance hired us. If they want someone else to guard the vase, I've got nothing to say about it." He strode off. "I'm going to find out why they've taken it back and where they're going to keep the vase."

I took a breath. "Something's not right."

We entered the village, and Parrot nodded toward the

ceremonial hut, where Jaaci stood in the entryway, waving us over. "Dinnertime," Parrot said. "Let's go."

"*Great.* Wonder what's on the menu tonight? Roasted armadillo? Sautéed rat? Grilled bobcat?" Feeling a bit whiny about the whole food issue, I followed Parrot across the village.

Someone had lit the outside torches, casting the area in a campsite glow. We stepped into the ceremonial hut, and I immediately noticed that Talon's stool was empty, as well as that of a chief who occupied the seat two down from him and the Huworo chief. Parrot and Jonathan noticed, too.

The guys went their way, and with dread I took my spot beside Jaaci along the back wall. I sighed, feeling like this had been one of the longest days of my life. Actually, yesterday had been long, too.

Quietly, I sat watching women bring food in and set it on the big round table in the middle. I eyed the platters, trying to make out the food. Unlike the monkey stew, tonight's dinner had no smell.

Like before, everyone took their spots according to gender and age. The Huworo chief entered just in time to do the chanting prayer with his family. Then the women began leaving our area to serve their families. I tried to see what they served and made out something green and something else white. I waited for my turn, and following Jaaci, I went up to the center table.

A variety of vegetables had been spread across huge serving platters. I breathed a sigh of relief when I saw them. Something short and gray filled the serving bowls. I watched as Jaaci scooped the objects out and onto small plates.

It was probably bad manners, but I picked up one of the objects and inspected the ridged stubbiness of it.

What the . . . ? I blinked.

A grub?

# # #

THE NEXT MORNING I WOKE up starving because, *hello*, I didn't eat the grubs, and vegetables hold your stomach off for only so long. I did the morning bath ritual with the other single women. Breakfast consisted of fruit and fish, thank God, something I recognized.

I put my cloth bug pouch around my neck, got my laptop, and found Quirk outside the big ceremonial hut. Together we made our way through the jungle toward the cave. As we walked, I filled him in on what had happened the night before with Talon and the Huworo chief taking the vase.

When we got to the swinging bridge, my phone beeped, alerting me I had a signal.

"You go on ahead," I told Quirk. "My phone gets a signal here, so my laptop would, too. And I need to send something back to home base."

"Sure. Be careful, though. You really shouldn't be out here alone."

"I'll be fine."

With a nod, he continued on and I sat down beneath a tree. I powered up my computer and scanned the drawing of the mysterious woman. Although the sketch was in two pieces—thanks to my klutziness—I still managed to get a decent scan. I hooked up my foldable satellite dish and keyed in the scrambler code.

HI! Chapling typed.

I smiled. HI! SENDING U A PIC. I watched as my computer transferred the file to Chapling back at the ranch.

WOW! SHES HOT! he typed.

I laughed. CAN U FIGURE OUT WHO SHE IS?

I'LL GIVE IT A WHIIIRRRL. PEACE OUT.

I laughed again. PEACE OUT.

I logged off and closed my laptop, eager to get to the cave and Quirk. He was right, I really shouldn't be here alone.

"I could make good money off you."

I jerked my head up and froze, and my heart picked up its pace. "T-Talon," I stuttered, and then immediately realized I'd just shown my fear.

An evil smile crept into his face. "You know my name. I'm honored."

I swallowed and concentrated on slowing down my heartbeat, on not showing fear.

Dressed in a traditional breechcloth with no shirt, he folded his arms over his thick chest. Even though he stood five feet seven, his stance made him seem an intimidating seven feet tall. He leveled his dark eyes on me, and they reminded me of all the other bad guys I'd faced—soulless, evil, lacking a conscience. They made my skin crawl.

I swallowed again and focused on forming a complete sentence. "What are you doing here?"

"It is to your benefit that you translate those cave drawings to my benefit."

I glanced across the swinging bridge to where Quirk had gone, but didn't see him. I brought my gaze back to Talon's. Putting my laptop aside, I stood. At least then I would be taller than him.

Talon's face didn't change expression. "It is to *your* benefit that you translate these drawings to *my* benefit," he repeated.

"Are you threatening me?" I tried to come across calm, but even I detected the uneasiness in my voice.

He took a step toward me, and I lost my small sense of confidence. "Your distance keep." I shook my head. "I mean, keep your distance."

Talon's lip curled up with my show of nervousness. He took another step closer, knowing full well he had the advantage. "Do you value your friends' lives? Do you value your life?"

Swallowing, I nodded, wishing Quirk or Guillermo or Jonathan or *someone* would appear out of the jungle.

Talon took another step toward me. "Then you *will* falsify your findings. I want the vase."

I didn't answer. I didn't trust myself to speak.

He took another step, and I gave in and moved back, coming up against the tree. One more step for him and he stood mere inches from me. I looked down into his face trying so hard not to show my fear.

Talon ran his creepy gaze down my body and back up. "Yes, I could make some money off you."

My body began to tremble. "M-m-move away."

He leaned forward. "Good money."

I turned my face away, shaking so hard my entire body vibrated. Way back in the recesses of my mind, I knew I could overpower him. I'd been trained to. But I also knew that at this point overcoming my fear was pretty much hopeless.

Talon touched his finger to my windpipe. "You *will* do as I've asked." He applied pressure, and I coughed. "Women are useless. And smart women, even more." He applied slightly more pressure, and I gagged.

He could do anything to me right now, and no one would know. The realization hit me hard at the exact second he stepped back.

I kept my face turned away, and in my peripheral vision I saw him disappear back into the jungle.

With shaky relief that I was still alive, my body slumped at the base of the tree. I sat for a few minutes, taking deep breaths, fighting tears, getting my heart back in rhythm, going over everything that had just happened, and how I'd reacted so weakly.

All my training, all the confidence I'd gained during my time with the Specialists—gone in a moment. I hated myself.

I heard a rustle of leaves, and my heart jumped. Guillermo stepped from the jungle, and I let out a breath.

He held up his hands. "It's okay. It's just me. I saw everything that happened. I've been following Talon since last night."

Relief and then anger sparked in me. "Why didn't you help me?" God, I'd been so scared.

"I needed to see what would happen. What he'd say. What he'd do. I wouldn't have let him hurt you." Guillermo nodded to the swinging bridge. "I'm going to stand here and watch you until you get to the cave. Get Quirk and get back to the village. We need to have a meeting."

Grabbing up my stuff, I made my way as fast and safely as I could across the bridge. At the cave's entrance, I turned and waved to Guillermo, and he disappeared back into the jungle.

I checked my phone for a signal, hoping to have a quick call with David. I just needed to hear his voice. But I'd lost the temporary satellite transmission. With a sigh, I clipped my phone on my belt. I'd have to be strong and handle things on my own.

I crawled into the cave and told Quirk what happened. Together, we went back to the village, found the talks on a break, and saw our team waiting for us at the corral.

"He's violated every rule of the alliance," Guillermo spoke, obviously having already told Jonathan and Parrot what had happened. "This is enough to get him kicked out of the talks. But in doing that we won't know who he's working with to steal the vase. We know there is someone else, but we need proof."

Jonathan looked first at me and then Parrot. "Do *not* go anywhere unless you have someone with you."

We both nodded. "Yes, sir."

"Hannah, you need to get working on those cave-drawing translations. The faster we can know what those drawings say, the quicker we can end these talks. Have you found anything yet?"

"I'm working on it," I replied. "My program hasn't revealed

anything, but once I input more drawings, I should have some preliminary results."

"Good," Jonathan replied. "As for the vase, I've spoken to the Huworo chief. It is being kept at the lookout tower."

I craned my neck all the way up and saw the two bald guards standing post on the watchtower. Not a bad place to keep the vase.

"The chief had heard from one of his people that there have been more whispers about the vase being stolen. He felt that the vase would be safer up in the tower. While I disagree, I have no power to argue with him."

Quirk cleared his throat and, with a slight nod, indicated the ceremonial hut. My team turned to see Talon standing in the entryway watching us.

"Let's break up," Guillermo said, and he and Quirk strolled off.

"Jonathan," Parrot began, "it's very likely Talon knows who I am. If he does, that means he has the upper hand."

Talon knew Parrot would do anything for the truth about his mother. The question was, *would* Parrot really do anything?

"Yes," Jonathan agreed. "But he doesn't know what *we're* capable of."

12

QUIRK AND I spent the next day in the cave—he was drawing the glyphs and I was scanning them into my translation software. We worked for hours, and at the end of the day I *click-click-clicked*. But again, my program gave me nothing.

Quirk was beginning to doubt my software.

I was frustrated. I had hoped to have something by now, but some of the glyphs just weren't matching up. According to my program, there were at least a dozen possible translations, but I didn't want a dozen *possible* ones, I needed one real one. It made me feel a bit stupid, to tell you the truth. I'd failed at a lot of things, but never computers. I knew them better than I knew myself.

It was dark when Quirk and I finally exited the cave and headed back.

As we stepped from the jungle, we saw a frenzied village. The single women and girls were running around, talking fast, giggling, obviously excited about something.

I noticed they'd changed from their traditional clothes into more ceremonial-looking garments. They wore small skirts and short tops, with beads around their wrists, necks, and bare stomachs. Considering I'd seen them dressed primarily in knee-length, sleeveless dresses, the traditional bikini-looking clothing came as a total shock.

Eager to see what was going on, I hightailed it toward the ceremonial hut and ran straight into Guillermo.

"What's going on?" I asked.

"Some of the chiefs have bowed out," he said as a greeting.

"What happened?"

"Through the course of the talks they've realized their tribes have no claim to the Mother Nature vase. They headed home earlier today."

"Is Talon one of them?" I hoped beyond hope.

"No, and he's been very 'well behaved' today. He's done nothing out of the ordinary. He didn't go anywhere or do anything he wasn't supposed to." Guillermo narrowed his eyes. "He's up to something."

Out of the corner of my eye, I caught sight of some girls hurrying into the ceremonial hut. I nodded toward them. "What's going on?"

"Full moon harvest dance."

I blinked. "Full moon what?"

"It's to ensure a prosperous harvest. It's the Huworo custom." Guillermo nodded to the ceremonial hut. "Let's go. It's an honor to attend this ceremony."

Torches had been lit to illuminate the night village. I followed Guillermo across and into the ceremonial hut. Things had been rearranged. Instead of the women sitting along the back, the men and chiefs occupied that area. The women sat right in front of the men. Everything had been cleared from the middle.

The teen girls stood in a large circle facing inward, and the teen guys surrounded them facing outward. In the middle of them all, a fire flickered. Like the girls, the guys had changed for the event into a small bikini bottom. They wore identical red-and-yellow stripes painted down their faces and bare chests.

Guillermo gave my arm a slight pull and led me over to Jonathan, Parrot, Jaaci, and Quirk, who were standing in an empty space along the back wall.

The same chief who had chanted at each meal stood, and the entire hut fell silent. Carrying a thick piece of wood with feathers tied on both ends, he strode to the center of the hut and came to a stop in front of one of the guys.

Bowing his head, the guy went down on both knees in front of the chief. The chief touched his feathered staff to the guy's right shoulder, then left, then his head, and then ran the staff down both of his arms. The chief closed his eyes and chanted something in his language.

"What's he saying?" I whispered to Parrot.

"That guy is the oldest single male," Parrot translated. "He'll lead the dance. The chief is praying for a good harvest."

Jonathan cleared his throat, his way of telling us to be quiet.

The chief finished the prayer, reared back with the staff, and slammed it right into the guy's chest.

I cringed.

The guy didn't even flinch. He jumped to his feet with an adrenaline-filled yell.

An old man whom I hadn't seen before entered the hut, banging his palm against a drum propped under his arm.

Immediately the girls and guys moved, circling in opposite directions with their backs to each other. Linking fingers, the girls closed their eyes, lifted their faces upward, and began singing a high-pitched song.

At that second the moon beamed in through the opening in the top of the ceremonial hut, illuminating the girls' faces.

The old man with the drum wove his way around the hut, taking oversize slow steps as he beat out a rhythm. *Ba. Ba. Badadaba. Ba. Ba. Badadaba . . .*

The chief shouted something, and, keeping their eyes closed and faces lifted, all the girls turned to face the guys' backs. The girls linked fingers again and continued circling, singing their high-pitched song.

Ba. Ba. Badadaba. Ba. Ba. Badadaba . . .

The guys linked arms at their elbows and began a deep guttural chant. Unlike the girls, their eyes stayed open, but they kept their gazes fixed to the ground.

Ba. Ba. Badadaba. Ba. Ba. Badadaba . . .

Everyone in the hut started chanting as the girls and guys circled faster and faster. The whole ceremony was powerful and gave me chills as I watched it unfold.

The chief raised the staff above his head, and slowly circling it in the air, he chanted something in the Huworo language. The girls and guys broke apart from their circles and all the older men and women sitting along the hut's perimeter got up. The old man continued banging the drum, and everyone, except the visiting chiefs, started dancing.

A couple minutes ticked by, and as I watched, I realized each person's awkward dancing maintained a unique rhythm.

The old man drummer crossed in front of us, and the Huworo chief danced toward us. He came to a stop right in front of Jonathan and said something. We all looked at Parrot.

"It's his wish that we join the dance," Parrot translated.

"No, thank you," I immediately replied.

"It would be considered a slap in his face," Guillermo put in, "if we don't participate." He looked at Jonathan. "We don't want to offend him."

"I'll do it." Quirk shot away from us as if he'd been dying for the invitation and joined the mass of dancing bodies, gyrating in his own unusual version of the dance.

Jonathan nodded to the chief. "It's our honor to participate."

Parrot translated, and with a satisfied smile, the chief writhed his way back into the group. Guillermo followed, and Jonathan looked at Parrot and me.

"Consider it part of your training," Jonathan rationalized.

Parrot and I gave each other matching looks of dread with an underlying hint of *how do we get out of this?*

Jonathan probably saw our wheels turning because he arched a disciplinary brow. "Do it." With that, he left our side and joined the seizuring bodies.

Jaaci stepped in front of both of us. With a sweet smile, she took my hand and then Parrot's and led us into the throng.

Dropping our hands, she spun away and into the crowd.

I turned to Parrot to say, "Well, here goes nothing," but found him standing with his eyes closed. His face appeared meditative as his body began to sway, absorbing the beat of the drum.

Without opening his eyes, he stepped forward into the group and began his dance.

I'd never seen Parrot so lost in his own personal moment. It made me wonder if he'd performed a ritual dance similar to this one in his pre-Specialist life

Someone bumped into me, and I realized I was the only one *not* moving. All around me people gyrated to the old man's drum, and without another thought, I joined in. Throwing my arms up I did what I labeled "whatever" moves. The dance was perfect for someone uncoordinated like me. It took on no style.

As I was getting into the rhythmic beat of the drum, I heard a voice rise above the music.

"*Kipbup!*"

A few people stopped dancing.

"*Kipbup!*"

More people stopped.

Someone screamed.

I spun around and saw one of the guards standing in the entrance covered in blood.

13

CHAOS BROKE OUT. Women screamed, men ran from the hut, and I frantically looked around for my team.

Parrot and Quirk quickly came up right beside me.

"What going on?"

"*Kipbup* means murder," Parrot said. "Someone's been murdered."

"*What?!*" I looked around and saw Jonathan running toward us.

"Stay here," he ordered as he and Guillermo raced past us.

I glanced around the hut, trying to recall who I had seen, who'd been missing from the harvest dance, who could possibly be dead. I caught sight of Jaaci and breathed a sigh of relief. She could very easily be a target.

Outside I heard a woman's wail, and it brought cold prickles to my skin. "Who died?"

Parrot shook his head. "I don't know yet. But it looks like the guard tried to save the person."

More people hurried from the hut as others came back in. Then Jonathan reappeared, motioning us out.

Quirk, Parrot, and I followed Jonathan out of the hut. Many

of the Huworo people had gathered at the base of the tree where the watchtower was. I looked all the way up . . .

And sucked in a breath.

Covered in blood, one of the guards dangled by a rope around his neck. His body swayed in the air as a couple of Huworo men slowly pulled him up onto the watchtower's platform.

I put my hands over my mouth. "Oh, my God."

"Come on," Jonathan said, directing us into the jungle. We walked in silence and about a quarter of a mile in, came to a stop. From his backpack he pulled three pieces of wood that had been shaped into knives. He gave one to each of us. "Keep this on you at all times. Don't be afraid to use it. And do *not* trust anyone."

I took my knife and knew without a doubt in my mind I would use it if I had to.

"Listen to me," Jonathan emphasized. "These hand-carved knives are *extremely* sharp and dangerous. Only use them if absolutely necessary." He looked at me and Quirk. "You two, I don't want you coming out of that cave until you know what those glyphs say."

We nodded. "Yes, sir."

Jonathan turned to Parrot. "Don't leave the village."

Parrot nodded his understanding.

Back to the village we went. Quirk and I packed up enough food and water to get us through the next twenty-four hours. With renewed determination, I knew, without a doubt in my mind, that I would figure out the ancient code.

One person had died. There was no telling what would happen next. That dangling guard could have been any one of my team members.

In the dark, Jonathan escorted us to the cave. "I'll check on you when I can. Guillermo will try to keep a watch on the cave entrance as well. I wish I had more people. Someone to post outside the entrance at all times."

"We'll be fine," I reassured him.

With a nod, he headed off.

Inside the cave we illuminated the lanterns. I plugged a new battery into my laptop and powered up. While Quirk began working, I analyzed every line of code in my program. . . .

<kso=^9# +lqy-#0!>

<\alt ~7s, nqk=.?"@>

<`bamo {77%%} [1]>

"Here," Quirk threw something at me, jarring me from my concentration.

I looked at the foil-wrapped rectangular object. "A PowerBar? Where did you get a PowerBar in the jungle?"

"I packed it in my luggage. But clearly you need it more than me." Quirk handed me a sketch.

How sweet of him to bring me a PowerBar. It reminded me of David, when he brought me lollipops.

Unwrapping the PowerBar, I took a bite, and Quirk and I dove back into our work. He sketched, I scanned, and hours ticked by. Vaguely, I registered Jonathan checking in on us.

Click, click, click . . . I stared blurry-eyed at the screen. . . . Seconds rolled by in sync with the script scrolling my monitor.

"Well?" Quirk leaned over my shoulder. "Anything?"

My heart gave a happy little pitter-patter. "We've gone from a dozen possible translations down to four. That's progress." *Major* progress.

Quirk nodded. "Definitely." He held his hand out to me and pulled me to my feet. "Let's take a one-minute stretch break and get back to work."

One minute later we were back at it again. He sketched faster than I'd ever seen him. I scanned, reorganized the data, and more hours ticked by. Again, I vaguely registered Jonathan checking in.

Click, click, click . . . I kept my eyes fastened to the screen. . . . "We've gone from four down to two." I glanced up at Quirk. "Almost there."

With a nod, he continued sketching. "You doing okay? Tired?"

I should have been, but pure adrenaline surged through my veins. "I'm fine. You?"

"Peachy."

I laughed a little at that.

Sometime later Quirk handed me a sketch. "That's the last one. It's all up to you now."

I scanned it and, tuning everything out, focused on my program. I changed the results of the docket, redefined the prequibble, and corresponded the conspecti with the raciocinata.

Hours later I *click, click, clicked* . . . and took what felt like my first breath since starting. "We've got it."

we packed up and headed back to the village. Sixteen hours had taken us into the early afternoon of the next day.

I found Parrot at the corral and stepped up beside him. My horse, Diablo, came right over. I gave his nose a pet.

"Well?" Parrot asked me.

"I've deciphered it."

He smiled. "I knew you would. I don't suppose you're going to tell me."

"I have to tell Jonathan first—by the way, where is he?"

"He'll be back in a few. He and Guillermo are having a meeting." Parrot pointed up to the watchtower. "New guard."

I glanced up. "What has happened since I've been gone?"

He let out an exhausted sigh. "Couple of chiefs got in an all-out fistfight. A few others have bowed out. There are still eight left, and none of them are budging on the quote/unquote proof the Mother Nature vase belongs to their tribe." Parrot shook his head. "And there was another attempt at stealing the vase."

"Oh, my God. Please tell me no one died this time."

"No. Jonathan was there to intercede."

"They should have just left him as the official guard to begin with." I glanced up at the watchtower again and experienced a quick image of that dangling body. "Who tried to steal it?"

"Believe it or not, one of the young girls."

"What?!"

Parrot shrugged. "I'll be glad when all this mess is over."

"You and me both. I can't wait to go home." Where lollipops, my bed, food, friends, and David were waiting.

"You can say that again." Parrot took a sip from a brown pottery mug.

"What are you drinking?"

"Cinnamon coffee. Jaaci gave it to me." He handed me the mug. "Try some. It's good."

I did. And it was.

We stood there in companionable silence, Parrot and I both petting the horses. Something moved behind us, and we both turned to see Talon approach.

Beside me Parrot visibly stiffened, and I whispered, "Relax. Don't let him see you're nervous."

Coming up right beside Parrot, Talon leaned his back against the corral. With a thin sliver of wood, he picked his teeth, all relaxed, like he was hanging out with his pals in the barnyard. "With your blue eyes, long hair, and beard, I almost didn't recognize you. Almost, Darren with the magic tongue."

Darren. I'd forgotten that was Parrot's real name.

Slowly, Parrot turned to face Talon. "What do you want?"

Talon sneered. "That's right. I still have information about your mother." He let out a pleasant sigh, making a sarcastic show of enjoying this. "What a pretty young girl she was. You two favor each other. Let's see"—he made a show of pondering—"her name was . . . Sarah. That's right, Sarah."

Parrot took a step forward, and I knew he was about to blow.

Talon made a *tsk*ing noise. "Poor little Sarah. Or should I call her by her new name, Sparrow. What a sad life she led. Sold into slavery. Little Sparrow was quite popular among the slave trade."

"*What?!*" Parrot shouted. "Where is she?"

Talon smirked. "Well, I'm going to need something if you want that kind of information."

I stepped up. "I'm not falsifying my findings."

Talon shrugged. "That's nice, but I still want the vase, and that's what I'll have." Talon flicked his toothpick aside. "Meet me back here tonight. Midnight. You don't have the vase, I'll give the order that your mother be killed."

"How are we supposed to get the vase?"

Talon sneered. "Sounds like your problem, not mine." He glanced up at the watchtower and sighed. "Too bad one of the guards had to die. If he would've just handed over the vase like I'd asked—"

"Did you kill him?" Oh, my God.

"I didn't say that, now, did I?" Talon looked straight at me. "I do have many loyal people who work for me. People willing to do anything."

Hit men, but I didn't say it. I grabbed Parrot's arm. "Let's go." With all my strength I pulled him away.

"I always thought she left," he said when we were out of ear-shot from Talon. "I didn't know Talon sold her into slavery."

I rubbed Parrot's back. "And you still don't know. He could be lying. It's no wonder TL's had problems finding her. If her name has been changed, and she is in some sort of slave ring, there's no telling how many times she's been sold and resold. How many times her name has been changed."

With a moan, Parrot covered his face with his hands, and I realized I'd probably been too graphic with the possible details of his mom's situation.

Jonathan emerged from the jungle as we passed by the single-men hut. "What's wrong?" he asked.

I looked at Parrot and his clenched jaw, and I knew he wasn't opening it to explain. I turned to Jonathan. "Talon alluded to the fact he killed the guard or possibly hired a hit man to do it. And he told us to steal the vase and meet him at the corral at midnight."

"Or?" Jonathan asked.

I put my arm around Parrot. "Or he'd give the order for Parrot's mom to be killed."

Jonathan looked right at Parrot. "Your mom is not going to die. We'll play Talon's game, but our way. We're meeting him at midnight."

\# \# \#

I LAY WIDE AWAKE IN my hammock, incessantly checking my watch.

11:11 P.M.

I went over everything in my head that Jonathan had planned. We'd have a pouch with a fake vase. Parrot and I would use it as leverage in obtaining his mother's location. We'd give Talon the false artifact, and Jonathan and Guillermo would move in.

11:23 P.M.

I listened to the night sounds. A symphony of bugs, frogs, and a million other jungle night crawlers filled the air. Jonathan, Guillermo, and Quirk would be watching from the woods the whole time. Nothing would go wrong.

11:39 P.M.

An occasional soft snore, heavy breath, or the sound of a body shifting filtered past me in the single-women hut.

11:51 P.M.

I swung my legs over the side of the hammock and, with a deep breath, left the hut. I crossed the village, squinting toward the corral. Through the night I made out the shadows of the horses as they restlessly moved around.

I saw a person standing inside the corral holding a long object. And then another person beside him.

As I passed the ceremonial hut, something moved in my peripheral vision, and I turned to see Parrot coming toward me, holding the pouch with the fake vase.

I waited for him to catch up. "There's someone with Talon."

Parrot's gaze flicked to the corral. "That's the leader from Southern Mexico. Looks like we know who the other bad chief is."

I nodded toward the corral, absolutely determined Talon would not intimidate me this time. "Let's do this."

We approached the corral fence. The horses shifted with agitation at having Talon and the other chief inside the area.

Diablo and Abrienda tried to come over and say hi to us, but

Parrot held his hand up and shook his head, and, surprisingly, the horses kept their distance.

Talon nodded to the pouch. "I'm not even going to ask how you got that away from the guards." He smirked. "Aren't you just sly these days?"

My gaze switched to a long spear Talon held in his hand. "What did you bring that for?" I asked, proud of my gutsy voice.

Talon shrugged. "Never know when you might need a good spear."

I didn't like that answer.

"I'm not into dramatics." Talon held out his hand. "Toss the pouch here, and I'll tell you where your mother is."

I put my hand on Parrot's arm. "Doesn't work that way. You tell us where his mom is, and we'll give you the pouch."

Talon narrowed his eyes.

"And," I continued with my bold ultimatum, "you lie to us about his mom, and you suffer. I think you've figured out by now that we have the ability to make you do just that. We have access to top secret things. Things you could only dream of." I pinned him with the stealthiest gaze I'd seen TL do. "You will be hunted down, both of you, and made to suffer.

"And, you lay one finger on my friend, and the same applies." Because once the location of Parrot's mom was revealed, he'd be free to testify against Talon. Talon knew that. Maybe that's why he'd brought the spear. To end Parrot's life.

Silence fell over us as my threat lingered in the air. I concentrated on not swallowing, blinking, or moving. I kept my icy eyes on Talon, letting him see every ounce of the truth in what I'd said. Somewhere in the back of my mind, I knew I'd gone too far, but I also knew I'd carry out the threat if need be.

The chief beside Talon swallowed, and the sound gurgled in the air. The nervous reaction pleased me.

Talon grunted. "Darren will not testify against me."

"Done," Parrot immediately agreed. "Tell me where my mother is."

"Poland. The city of Racpap. On Nublin Street. Number Twenty-three." Talon held his hand out for the vase, and Parrot tossed it to him.

Like two greedy boys, the chiefs eagerly untied the pouch and began unwrapping the thick layers of protective cloth.

Parrot and I turned away and started back across the village.

"Racpap. Nublin Street. Twenty-three," he recited. "Racpap. Nublin Street. Twenty-three."

"Pick up your pace," I whispered. "Talon's about to discover the vase is fake."

"WHAT IS THIS?!" Talon yelled through the night.

Parrot and I took off running. We wove through the village, dodging behind huts, jumping gardens, and disappeared into the jungle. Hearts pounding, we ran as fast as we could through the dark to the river. Plants slapped us, thorns stabbed us, limbs tripped us, but we kept going.

Minutes later we emerged at the river, our predetermined meeting place.

Gasping for air, I braced my hands on my knees. "Jonathan"— I took a breath—"and Guillermo"—I took another breath—"should have got him by now."

Sucking in air, Parrot nodded.

Out of the corner of my eye, a shadowed figure emerged from the jungle. I jerked up.

The Huworo chief stepped onto the river's bank. He said something in his language and nodded to the right.

"He says," Parrot translated, "he saw everything that happened. And this is not a safe place. Talon is heading right toward us."

"But what about Jonathan?"

Parrot turned to the Huworo chief, asked him that question, and the chief responded.

Parrot didn't say anything at first. He didn't even look at me.

"What?" I nearly shouted.

Parrot rubbed his hands down his face. "Oh, my God."

"WHAT?!"

"The chief says Jonathan has been killed and Guillermo's been seriously injured."

My whole body went numb. "Wh-what?" I shook my head. "That can't be."

Jonathan's words echoed in my brain. *If anything happens to me . . .*

The Huworo chief said something.

"He says," Parrot translated, "that we have to hurry. Talon's very close."

I shook my head again. *Something's not right.* "I want to see his body. I don't believe he's dead."

Something rustled in the jungle, and the chief took off running.

Parrot grabbed my arm and raced after the chief down the bank of the river. Tugging my arm free, I kept up the pace, glancing back every now and then to where we'd come from. The river cut around a corner, and I lost track of where we were.

The clouds parted, and the nearly full moon lit up the area.

More of Jonathan's words echoed through my brain. *Don't trust anybody. . . .*

My breath hitched with the overwhelming emotion. Jonathan was dead. TL was on another continent. David, too. Guillermo was seriously injured. And I had no idea where Quirk was.

Breathe, GiGi, breathe.

I still had Parrot, I reminded myself.

The chief darted off into the jungle, and we followed. The foliage surrounded us, blocking out any meager rays of moonlight. I tripped over something and felt Parrot pulling me up. He ran into a tree, and I was there to catch him. We both rolled down a bank and helped each other up. I tasted blood. With the amount of things scraping my face, there was no telling where it was coming from.

An animal roared through the night, and my already pounding heart leapt.

Oh, my God. We're going to die.

Right as that thought went through my brain, we emerged at the swinging bridge that spanned the canyon and led to the cave.

Sucking in air, Parrot and I looked around.

The chief said something. I turned in his direction and stumbled backward mere inches from the canyon's edge.

Holding a gun at me and Parrot, the chief repeated what he'd said.

"He says," Parrot gulped a breath, "that we either end our lives in the canyon or he's going to shoot."

"What?" I caught my sob. *Don't trust anybody. . . .* "Oh, my God." And then I started crying.

Parrot wrapped his arm around my shoulders.

"Lower the gun," a voice spoke to my left, and I jerked around.

Quirk stood at the border of the jungle with a rifle pointed straight at the Huworo chief. A shadow emerged behind him. I recognized the figure a split second before I screamed, "Quirk!"

And then everything happened lightning quick. Raising a rock high above his head, Talon slammed it down on Quirk's skull, and he fell flat on his face. Talon brought his spear back and slung it through the air, and with a squish, it pierced the Huworo chief's chest, sending him sailing through the dark into the canyon. Then Talon swung Quirk's rifle up into his hands and pointed it right at me and Parrot.

Neither one of us moved.

He cocked the rifle, making it more than apparent he wasn't talking, just shooting. I shoved Parrot away from me and dove in the opposite direction at the exact second Talon fired.

The booming sound echoed through the canyon and vibrated my body. Immediately, I recalled what Jonathan had said during PT.

What is my objective? To disable Talon.

What is my terrain? A canyon behind me, jungle in front.

Is there an enemy nearby? Yes.

Is there a team member nearby? Yes. One alive, one now unconscious.

How much time do I have to meet my objective? ASAP.

What resources do I have at my disposal? Dirt, rocks, my knife, canyon, swinging bridge.

With that thought, I grabbed a handful of rocks and dirt and slung it at Talon.

With a string of curses, he wiped his eyes, and I used that opportunity to move. I pulled my knife from the back of my pants and threw it in his direction.

He roared out in pain, and his face slowly morphed into an evil I didn't think I'd ever seen before. Like something else had taken over his body. With a deep, guttural scream, he pulled my knife from his thigh, nailed me with his possessed eyes, and raised the knife high above his head. Blood dripped from the tip down his face. With an inhuman grunt, he charged me.

I dodged to the right a split second too late. The knife grazed my side, and I hissed in a breath.

Talon laughed.

"Leave her alone!" Parrot yelled. "It's me you want."

Talon laughed again right as the moonlight disappeared, plunging us into darkness. I heard his evil chuckle as he scurried away from me.

I stayed very still and quiet as my eyes adjusted to the night, and I searched every shadow, trying to see where Talon had gone. I made out a figure to my right and narrowed my gaze. I watched as Parrot stealthily climbed a tree, lifted his knife above his head, and then leapt. I heard two bodies collide, and Talon's grunt echoed through the night.

I couldn't figure out where Parrot's knife had gone. If he'd injured Talon. If Talon had knocked the knife away.

I raced toward them as they rolled across the ground, coming up against the swinging bridge. Talon got on top, and I saw a jagged cut crisscross his back. He brought his fist up and slammed it into Parrot's jaw.

Parrot kneed him in the side, gaining top ground. He brought his fist back and nailed Talon in the mouth. A chunk of white flew through the air, and I hoped it was Talon's tooth.

I searched the ground, looking for a rock or any sort of weapon. I caught sight of Parrot's knife, grabbed the wooden handle, and lunged toward them. Parrot shifted, and I brought the knife down, jamming its jagged edge into Talon's shoulder.

He growled as he yanked my hair and slung me over him, and I smacked onto the bridge. With a scream I jumped to my feet, spun, and rammed the heel of my boot into Talon's head. At the same time Parrot jabbed his elbow into Talon's throat. Parrot lifted his forehead, ready for a head butt—

"Stop," I told him.

Parrot froze.

"He's out."

Neither one of us moved for a second.

Then slowly Parrot lifted off, and the two of us stood looking down at Talon. His thick body lay sprawled half on the bridge, half on the ground. Blood trickled from his eye, his mouth, and a gash in his forehead. Dirt and mud smeared his chest, arms, and legs.

I stepped over him. "We need to find something to tie him up with."

Parrot slid the knife from his shoulder. "I'll watch him. You go."

I hurried over to the jungle's edge and got down on my hands and knees, searching for long weeds, big leaves, anything to tie Talon up until we dragged him back to the village. My fingers connected with a thick vine. "Got something!"

With all my strength I dragged it from the thick overgrowth, turned, saw Parrot glance over his shoulder at me, and at the same time Talon lifted up. "PAAARRROOOTTT!"

Talon grabbed Parrot's ankle and yanked, sending him off balance, toppling over the canyon's edge.

"NOOO!" I screamed.

Parrot's horse, Abrienda, shot out from the jungle, and I stumbled away. I caught a glimpse of Jonathan on her back and nearly passed out.

Jonathan leaped off Abrienda and took off in the direction Parrot had gone. The horse reared up on her hind legs right over Talon, coming down only inches from his face.

He screamed and punched and kicked, grabbed fistfuls of dirt and rock, and threw it at her.

Baring her teeth, Abrienda let out a crying whinny, kicked out her front hooves, and came right down on top of him.

The sounds of bones crunching echoed through the night, and I cringed.

My horse, Diablo, flew right past me, and I caught a glimpse of Guillermo on his back.

I scrambled over to Jonathan, Guillermo, and the spot where I'd seen Parrot last. Guillermo was directing my horse, Diablo, back. Gripping a rope in his teeth, my horse slowly inched back, pulling with all his might at the rope. On his belly, Jonathan reached over the ledge and latched on to Parrot's forearm.

I stretched out right beside Jonathan and grabbed whatever I could on Parrot as Jonathan and Diablo pulled him up.

When I saw Parrot's bloody face, I burst into happy tears. As soon as his body was clear, I grabbed on. And somewhere in the recesses of my subconscious I registered Jonathan hugging us both.

14

TURNED OUT THE Huworo chief was the hit man, hired by Talon to kill anyone who stood in the way of his getting the Mother Nature vase.

Talon's coconspirator, the Southern Mexican chief, was taken away. He would stand trial with the alliance for sabotaging the talks. Apparently, he was involved in Talon's slave trade, too, and would stand trial in six different countries for his crimes.

Jonathan had given the information concerning Parrot's mom to TL. And that was all we knew at this point.

The Huworo chief had told us Jonathan died and Guillermo was seriously injured. Obviously, that was a lie. Apparently, the Huworo chief had shot them with sleeping darts, and they'd been unconscious for a while.

And now here Quirk and I stood the next afternoon in front of all the other chiefs. A white, gauzy bandage covered the back of Quirk's head where ten stitches had been put in.

We had the final glyph translation of the ancient code and were about to reveal it.

And I suspected *no one* was going to be happy.

Since we would be speaking English, Parrot wasn't needed for the chiefs. He sat in the back near Jaaci to translate for her. Besides my team members, she was the only nonchief allowed in this meeting.

"Good afternoon, gentlemen," Quirk greeted them.

All the chiefs' personal assistants leaned in and whispered the translation in their leader's ear.

"As you all know, I and my assistant"—Quirk indicated me—"have been working in the cave for the past days sketching the drawings, researching, and coming up with a translation. We were hired to give you the translation. What you do with it is up to the alliance." Quirk smiled. "And we are very pleased to have broken the ancient code."

He paused for the translators. . . .

"The code was supposed to reveal a key piece of information about the vase, and, as suspected, that key piece of information deals with the ownership of the Mother Nature vase."

The translators whispered. It may have been my imagination, but it seemed as if every chief in the hut leaned forward, waiting for the answer.

"The owner of the Mother Nature vase is"—Quirk paused—"the Muemiraa tribe."

Translation occurred, and everyone began speaking at once. Clearly, no one was happy.

He held his hand up to let them know he had more to say. Slowly, the hut quieted.

"As we all know, Jaaci is the only remaining member of the Muemiraa tribe." Quirk looked at Jaaci. "So she is the owner of the vase."

Parrot translated to Jaaci, and her eyes widened in complete disbelief.

Quirk nodded to me, and I took that as my cue to finish.

"The code also revealed that the person granted ownership of the Mother Nature vase will be deemed a prince or princess." I looked at Jaaci again. "In this case, a princess."

Parrot gave Jaaci the translation, and she looked across the hut at me in stunned amazement.

I could only imagine what I'd feel like if I'd just found out I was a princess. And the owner of a centuries-old artifact.

"Lastly," I continued, "based on documented proof, a century ago the Muemiraa tribe split, forming the Iokojoja people. That makes Jaaci, through her blood connections, a member of the Iokojoja people. She is a princess of the Iokojoja people."

Translation occurred, and my gaze went straight to Jaaci. I was happy for her. She had a family again. A real family. With bloodlines that traced back centuries.

I'd give anything for that.

⠿ ⠿ ⠿

THE CHIEFS MET AFTER WE left the ceremonial hut, deciding if they would accept our translation of the ancient code. Roughly thirty minutes later they had.

That afternoon, all the chiefs, along with my team, Quirk, and Guillermo, escorted Jaaci to the river. The same river we had bathed in every morning.

Quirk served as the official recorder, sketching the scenes and detailing in words the historical events taking place.

All the chiefs and Jaaci were dressed in beautiful ceremonial garb. Some wore enormous headdresses, others intricate breast-plates, and still others had their entire bodies decorated with paint.

And Jaaci . . . she wore her hair long and loose, and her white leather dress hung all the way to the ground with a slight train, as if she was getting married.

Parrot couldn't take his eyes off her. Heck, I couldn't either.

I'd heard the words *ethereal* and *celestial* before, but I'd never truly understood their meaning until now. Until looking at Jaaci.

In sequence, old to young, all the chiefs said a prayer in their language. I supposed they were blessing the vase as they passed it around, handing it finally to Jaaci.

Closing her eyes, she raised it above her head, saying her own prayer.

Goose bumps popped on my skin as I listened to her.

In a handwoven cloth, Jaaci wrapped the vase and carried it down to the river, where a canoe waited with the Iokojoja chief and his family. Turning, she bowed to all of us, and we silently watched as the canoe backed away from the shore. Parrot had told me their tribe lived a day's trip away on the river.

After they disappeared from sight, we all trekked through the jungle back to the village, and hours later, the chiefs and their assistants packed up and left. My team packed as well.

"Hannah," Quirk called me over as Jonathan and Guillermo were double-checking everything packed on the horses.

I followed him behind one of the huts.

"I wasn't sure if we'd get any privacy, so I just wanted to tell you I really enjoyed working with you."

I smiled. "Me, too. Who knows, maybe we'll be on another mission sometime."

He smiled back. "Maybe."

And then before I knew what was happening, he leaned in and gave me a kiss. "Thanks for 'getting' me."

Dumbfounded, I stood there, staring into his green eyes. He'd just kissed me.

"Um." He took a step back. "I—I can't believe I just kissed you." He let out a shaky laugh. "Oh, boy."

He'd just kissed me.

"Oh, boy. Are you okay?"

I gave my head a little shake and managed a wobbly smile. "Yes." And then I did something totally unexpected. I told him my real name. "My name's Kelly."

"Kelly," he said my name. "I'm Randy."

We both smiled.

He held out his hands. "Okay." And with a nod, Quirk/Randy walked right past me back toward the village.

I turned and watched him walk away, and David popped into my mind. Oh, my God. What would he think?

Quirk/Randy had kissed me. He'd really kissed me. I touched my fingers to my lips, and my stomach butterflied. His lips had felt soft and warm. David's lips were soft and warm, too . . . yet different. What did the kiss mean exactly? It had felt nice. Different. And Randy was right. I did "get" him. Just like he got me.

Should I tell David? My great *boyfriend*?

Yes, I probably should. I couldn't keep something like that from him. He'd tell me if some other girl had kissed him, right?

"Hannah," Jonathan yelled, interrupting my thoughts. "Let's go."

Suddenly, the urgency to get home doubled. I longed to see David.

▓ ▓ ▓

IT TOOK US THREE DAYS to horseback our way from the jungle and hop a couple of different planes from the country of Rutina back to America. A canceled flight, an extended layover in Dallas, and finally we arrived back in San Belden, California. Home. Guillermo had stayed in South America, and Randy had gone his own way in Dallas.

It was 1:00 in the morning when we arrived at the ranch. I couldn't wait to fall in the bed and sleep for eternity.

Jonathan nodded to the elevator. "TL wants to see us."

Parrot and I exchanged a tired glance.

With a yawn, I stepped onto the elevator. The door closed and we began descending. Four floors down we stepped off and followed Jonathan to the conference room, where TL stood waiting. He gave us a both a hug as we entered, and I sighed. I was home.

Parrot and I sat right beside each other, our chairs touching, our bodies as close as possible. We'd bonded in a way deeper than I'd connected with any of my other team members. Maybe it was because it had been just Parrot and me out there on the ledge, mere inches away from falling to our death. I'd been in dangerous situations before, but I'd always known TL or David or someone was nearby. Not this time, though. I'd truly believed that Jonathan was dead and that Parrot and I were on our own.

Parrot had almost died.

With that thought, a chill went through my body, and I reached under the table and clasped his hand. He grabbed on to mine tight as if he'd been thinking and feeling the same things.

Closing the door, TL came to sit in his seat at the table's head. For a few seconds all he did was survey our faces, taking in our bruises and cuts.

"I know the shaman of the Huworo tribe doctored you up, but I want both of you to see Dr. Gretchen first thing in the morning. I've instructed her to give you a complete physcial."

"Yes, sir," we responded.

"I want both of you to know how very proud I am of the job you've done. You've each far exceeded my expectations." TL turned to Parrot, his expression softening a bit. "I have news on your mother."

Parrot straightened in his chair.

"The address information Talon gave you was inaccurate. No surprise there. But her slave name, Sparrow, was correct. We confiscated the personal files of Talon's partner, the Southern Mexican chief. Using the information we found there, we were able to locate your mother. She will be here in the States in a few days."

Parrot let out a breath, like he couldn't quite believe what TL had just said. "Is she okay?"

"She's extremely malnourished. So when you see her, you need to be prepared. It's been ten years. A lot changes in a person in that time."

Nodding, Parrot dropped his gaze, trying to hide the tears welling in his eyes. Under the table I squeezed his hand again, so pleased for him.

TL turned to me. "How's your side?"

I put my hand over the gash that had been stitched and bandaged. "Fine." I wanted to ask him when David was due back, but figured this wasn't the appropriate time.

"Get some rest." TL gave us both a small smile. "You both need it." He glanced over his shoulder at Jonathan, who still stood at the door. "If you don't mind staying for a few minutes . . ."

Jonathan nodded.

Parrot and I made our way back up to the ranch level and split apart when we got to our rooms. Quietly, I opened the door to the girl's dormitory room and tiptoed in. Cat, Beaker, and Bruiser were fast asleep. I dropped my stuff on the floor next to my bed, changed clothes, did my thing in the bathroom, and dropped onto my mattress. I lay there for a few minutes with my eyes closed, listening . . . to the *quiet*. No bug noises. No frogs. No night crawlers. It was amazing how loud the jungle really was . . . and how quiet the nonjungle really was . . . and how, believe it or not, I'd gotten so used to the jungle noises. I sort of missed them.

Maybe I'd download a few of those nature songs to listen to at night. With a content smile and sigh, I felt my whole body relax and fell right to sleep. . . .

"*GiGi.*"

Somewhere far away in the jungle my name echoed. A big bug fluttered past my arm, and I brushed it away.

"*GiGi.*"

I grumbled. "I don't want to bathe."

"*GiGi.*"

"Whaaat?"

Something closed over my mouth, and my eyes shot open at the same time I executed a wonka-jonk, Bruiser's term for her version of the karate chop.

The person above me blocked my wonka-jonk and quietly pinned me to the hammock—er, um, bed. That's right, I was in a bed. In my home. Back at the ranch.

Through the dark I blinked my eyes real hard and focused in on the face above me . . . David!

His eyes crinkled when he realized *I* realized who he was.

"Oo ot pose to bee een ere," I mumbled into his hand.

David uncovered my mouth.

"You're not supposed to be in here," I whispered. He could get in major trouble if TL found him in here after curfew. But . . . who cared. David was here!

Putting his finger over his lips, he threw my covers back, took my hand, and led me from the room. Together we tiptoed down the dimly lit hall, past TL's door, through the cafeteria, and into the kitchen. With each step we took my heart banged harder and harder. Where were we going?

We crossed the kitchen, and David pulled open the door to the pantry. He led me inside and shut the door, plummeting us into darkness. This was the first place we'd ever kissed. And with that thought, I felt him move close.

"I heard a leech ate your butt." I could hear the humor in his voice, and I laughed.

He flicked a switch, and dim light illuminated the area. Like TL had done, David's gaze touched each of my bruises and cuts. I followed his eyes as they roamed over my cheeks, forehead, and chin. He reached out and carefully touched the spot on my side where'd I'd been knifed. And leaning forward, he gently pressed his lips to each mark on my face.

I closed my eyes and melted into his warmth, his strength, his familiarity.

He took a small step away, and from behind his back he brought out a lollipop. "Will this make things better?" he asked softly.

I smiled. "Always."

"Turn around," he said.

"What?"

He twirled his finger. "You heard me. Turn around."

With a quizzical look, I turned my back to him. I heard a slight rustling, and then David brought a necklace down in front of me and fastened it around my neck.

"What did you do?" I held out the silver emblem etched with odd writing.

He turned me back around. "It's a cartouche from Egypt. It's your name."

"David!" I hugged him. "It's beautiful. Thank you."

He smiled. "You're very welcome. It's your graduation gift."

"My what?"

"TL told me you graduated college. Congratulations."

"Oh. Thanks. Truthfully, I didn't graduate. I tested out of the last semester."

"Why didn't you tell me?"

"Don't know." I shrugged. "No big deal, really. Just another test."

"No big deal?" David raised his brows. "You're sixteen, and you graduated college."

"Almost seventeen."

"And you graduated college."

"Yeah? So?"

He stared at me with a perplexed look while I stared back.

Shaking his head, he chuckled and closed the minuscule space between us. "My God, I missed you." He backed me up against the door and covered my body with his. He started kissing me, and kissing me, and kissing me . . .

. . . *I'm so glad I'm wearing my cute pajamas* . . .

. . . and kissing me . . .

. . . Thank God I brushed my teeth . . .

. . . and kissing me . . .

. . . and I'm not even thinking about Quirk/Randy . . .

"You're thinking," he grumbled, leaving my mouth to nibble my neck.

He pressed soft kisses all over my face and neck and then picked up my hands and did them and my arms.

"How many kisses was that?" he asked.

"Hmmm . . . ?"

"You're supposed to be counting kisses, remember?"

How in the world did he expect me to remember that when I highly doubted I could conjure up the SAQ code right now? Oh, wait. I focused. No, I probably could.

"My bad. I made you think." He went straight for that part of my neck again, and my whole world spun.

"There." David chuckled. "Objective met."

▦ ▦ ▦

TWO DAYS LATER, I WAS in the garden pulling weeds, my chore for the day.

David stepped from the barn, caught sight of me, and came over. Kneeling beside me, he began helping.

"You don't have to do that," I told him.

He shrugged. "I know."

Together, we worked in silence and my thoughts drifted to Randy. They'd been doing that a lot since I'd gotten back.

"David?"

"Hm?"

"Would you tell me if another girl kissed you?"

David stopped working and looked up at me. "Why?"

I kept working, focusing so hard on the weeds, my eyes nearly crossed. "Because . . . because someone else kissed me." There. It was out. Finally.

My heart boinged around in my chest while I waited for his response.

"Who? Who kissed you?"

I kept working. "The glyph professor."

"Did he ask or did he just kiss you?" he asked, not sounding too happy.

"He just kissed me. But . . ." I didn't want him to think Randy had mistreated me or anything.

"But what?"

I kept working. "But nothing. It's just I didn't want you to think he'd forced me to kiss him or anything."

"So what are you saying?"

I didn't know how to answer that.

"Would you stop working, please?" he snapped.

I looked over at him. He did *not* look happy.

"What are you trying to say to me?" he repeated himself.

I took in his irritated face, thought of his wonderful heart, and felt like a complete idiot for bringing it up. "David," I sighed. "It didn't mean anything. You trust me, right?"

He jerked a nod.

And I decided to be completely honest with him. He deserved that. "The professor was cute and just a few years older and we . . . clicked, on an intellectual level. But I told him about you and how wonderful you are, and he completely respected that. And then when we said good-bye to each other, he gave me a quick kiss. I think the kiss surprised him as much as it did me, but that's all there was to it. He went his way, and I went my way, and that's that. And it's been bugging the heck out of me because I don't like keeping things from you. That's one of the good things about us. At the base of it all, we're friends."

I reached out and touched his arm. "I wouldn't do anything to hurt you."

"You don't think we click on an intellectual level?" His voice sounded so hurt, it made me feel horrible.

"Not like Chapling and I do."

"This professor guy was like Chapling?"

"Well, no, not exactly." God, I didn't know what to say to make things better.

David got up. "Let me just have some time to think."

"David," I said to his back as he walked away, but he didn't turn.

I tried to imagine how I would respond if the situation was reversed, and, truthfully, I'd probably be walking away right now, too.

A limo pulled through our security gate, drawing my attention away from David. It circled our driveway and came to a stop in front of the house. The driver got out and walked around to open the door for the passenger.

A tall, extremely skinny, dark-haired woman stepped out, wearing jeans and a long-sleeved blouse.

"Oh, my God," I realized out loud, "that's Parrot's mom."

The door to the house opened, and out came Parrot. He and his mom stood very still, staring at each other with only ten feet or so of space separating them.

My heart ached as I watched them.

They moved at once, running toward each other and colliding together. Even though I stood in the side yard, I could hear them crying.

Gripping each other tightly, they rocked each other and cried out the ten years they'd been apart.

The overwhelming emotion seem to ripple through the air as all my teammates slowly, quietly trickled out from wherever they were to witness the reunion.

I wondered how they all felt, having to watch this, feeling happy for Parrot, but wishing it for themselves, too.

I knew I wished it for myself.

And I wondered what this meant, if anything, for Parrot and his future with the Specialists.

TL approached them a few minutes later and said something. The two of them nodded, climbed in the limo, and pulled away.

Everyone slowly began trickling back to where they'd come

from, and TL turned in my direction. With two fingers he waved me over.

I jogged from the side yard across the driveway to the front. "Yes, sir?"

"Conference room. Now."

With a nod, I followed him into the house and down to Subfloor Four. We walked into the conference room, and I'd hoped David would be there.

"Hihihi!" Chapling greeted me instead.

I grinned. "Hi! I missed you." He'd been gone since I returned.

He giggled and leaned in. "Guess what," he whispered.

"What?"

"My mom got married again."

"Again?"

"Her eighth one." Chapling shrugged. "It shouldn't take long for her to move on to the ninth."

"*Eighth* marriage?" Holy sheesh. I realized then that I knew very little about Chapling's personal life. Mother, father, brothers, sisters, where he grew up . . . did he have a *girlfriend*?

Nah, somehow I couldn't see Chapling with a girlfriend.

"Chapling, do you realize I don't know anything about you?"

He fluttered his pudgy hand. "We'll purge our souls later."

TL shook his head. "You two get sidetracked so easily."

We both laughed at that.

TL looked at Chapling. "Why don't you tell her why we're really in here."

"Oh rightright." Chapling held up the sketch of the woman I'd stolen in South America. "I know who this is!"

I waited, but he didn't expound on the information. "Who?" I prompted.

"This is your sister."

"My *WHAT*?"

"Before your father joined the IPNC, he was married to another woman, and they had a daughter," TL responded. "Truthfully, I never even knew your father had had another wife. The daughter is fifteen years older than you."

I shook my head. "My father was married before my mother?" I hadn't known. *Obviously.* Or I wouldn't be so dumbfounded right now. "I have a-a-a *sister*?"

TL nodded. "Yes, you do."

"Wh-where?" I stammered.

TL shook his head. "We're not sure. But we're going to find her."

Don't forget to check out the next book in
THE SPECIALISTS series.

When someone close to TL disappears, The Specialists
pull out all the stops. GiGi is brought into another mission
along with Bruiser and Mystic. This time, it's a fight to the
end, and someone doesn't make it out alive.

WITHDRAWN

NMAADHTIM